Hippie

Paulo Coelho's life remains the primary source of inspiration for his books. He has flirted with death, escaped madness, dallied with drugs, withstood torture, experimented with magic and alchemy, studied philosophy and religion, read voraciously, lost and recovered his faith, and experienced the pain and pleasure of love. In searching for his own place in the world, he discovered answers for the challenges that everyone faces. He believes that, within ourselves, we have the necessary strength to find our own destiny.

His first novel, *The Alchemist*, has sold more than 85 million copies and has been cited as an inspiration by people as diverse as Malala Yousafzai and Pharrell Williams.

Paulo Coelho's books have sold more than 225 million copies worldwide and he is the most translated living author. He has won 115 international prizes and awards and in 2007 was named a United Nations Messenger of Peace.

Hippie

Paulo Coelho

arrow books

1 3 5 7 9 10 8 6 4 2

Arrow Books
20 Vauxhall Bridge Road
London SW1V 2SA

Arrow Books is part of the Penguin Random House group of companies whose
addresses can be found at global.penguinrandomhouse.com

Penguin
Random House
UK

First published in the United Kingdom by Hutchinson in 2018
First published in the United States by Knopf in 2018
First published in paperback by Arrow Books in 2019

www.penguin.co.uk

A CIP catalogue record for this book is available from the British Library.

ISBN 9781787461697
ISBN 9781787461710 (export)

Printed and bound in Great Britain by Clays Ltd, Elcograf S.p.A.

Penguin Random House is committed to a sustainable
future for our business, our readers and our planet.
This book is made from Forest Stewardship Council®
certified paper.

O Mary!
conceived without sin,
pray for us who turn to you!
Amen.

He was told, "Your mother and your brothers are standing outside and they wish to see you."

He said to them in reply, "My mother and my brothers are those who hear the word of God and act on it."

—LUKE 8:20–21

I thought that my voyage had come to its end
at the last limit of my power,
—that the path before me was closed,
that provisions were exhausted
and the time come to take shelter in a silent obscurity.
But I find that thy will knows no end in me.
And when old words die out on the tongue,
new melodies break forth from the heart;
and where the old tracks are lost,
new country is revealed with its wonders.

—RABINDRANATH TAGORE

For Kabir, Rumi, Tagore, Paulo de Tarso, Hafez,
Who have been with me ever since I first discovered them,
Who have written part of the story of my life,
Which I tell in the book that follows—often using their words.

The stories that follow come from my personal experiences. I've altered the order, names, and details of the people here, I was forced to condense some scenes, but everything that follows truly happened to me. I've used the third person because this allowed me to give characters unique voices with which to describe their lives.

Hippie ♥

In September 1970, two sites squared off for the title of the center of the world: Piccadilly Circus, in London, and Dam Square, in Amsterdam. But not everyone knew this: if you asked most people, they'd have told you: "The White House, in the US, and the Kremlin in the USSR." These people tended to get their information from newspapers, television, radio, media that were already entirely outdated and that would never regain the relevance they had when first invented.

In September 1970, airplane tickets were outrageously expensive, which meant only the rich could travel. OK, that wasn't entirely true for an enormous number of young people whom these outdated media outlets could see only for their outward appearance: they wore their hair long, dressed in bright-colored clothing, and never took a bath (which was a lie, but these young kids didn't read the newspaper, and the older generation believed any news item that served to denigrate those they considered "a danger to society and common decency"). They were a danger to an entire generation of diligent young boys and girls trying to succeed in life, with their horrible example of lewdness and "free love," as their detractors liked to say with disdain. Well, this ever-growing number of kids had a system for spreading news that no one, absolutely no one, ever managed to detect.

The "Invisible Post" couldn't be bothered to discuss the latest Volkswagen or the new powdered soaps that had just been launched around the globe. It limited its news to the next great trail awaiting exploration by those insolent, dirty kids practicing "free love" and wearing clothes no one with any taste would ever put on. The girls with their braided hair covered in flowers, their long dresses, bright-colored shirts and no bras, necklaces of all shapes and sizes; the boys with their hair and beards that hadn't been cut for months. They wore faded jeans with tears from overuse because jeans were expensive everywhere in the world— except for the US, where they'd emerged from the ghetto of factory workers and were worn at all the major open-air shows in and around San Francisco.

The "Invisible Post" existed because people were always going to these concerts, swapping ideas about where they ought to meet next, how they could explore the world without jumping aboard one of those tourist buses where a guide described the sights while the younger people grew bored and the old people dozed. And so, thanks to word of mouth, everyone knew where the next concert was to take place or where to find the next great trail to be explored. No one had any financial restrictions because, in this community, everyone's favorite author wasn't Plato or Aristotle or comics from some artist who'd attained celebrity status; the big book, which almost no one who traveled to the Old Continent did so without, went by the name *Europe on 5 Dollars a Day*. With this book, everyone could find out where to stay, what to see, where to eat, where to meet, and where to catch live music while hardly spending a thing.

Frommer's only error at the time was having limited his guide to Europe. Were there not perhaps other interesting places to see? Weren't there those who would rather go to India than to Paris? Frommer would address this failing a few years later, but until such time the "Invisible Post" took it upon itself to promote a South American itinerary ending at the once-"lost" city of Machu Picchu, with the warning not to mention anything to those who were outside of the hippie culture, lest the place be invaded by wild animals with cameras and extensive explanations (quickly forgotten) about how a band of Indians had created a city so well concealed it could be discovered only from above—something they considered impossible, since men did not fly.

Let's be fair: there was a second enormous bestseller, though not as popular as Frommer's book, which appealed more to those who had already flirted with socialism, Marxism, and anarchy; each of these phases always ended in deep disillusionment with the system invented by those who professed that "it was inevitable that the workers of the world would seize power." Or that "religion is the opium of the masses," which only proved that whoever uttered such a stupid statement understood little about the masses and even less about opium: among the things these poorly dressed kids believed in were God, gods, goddesses, angels, that sort of thing. The only problem is that the book, *The Morning of the Magicians,* written by the Frenchman Louis Pauwels and the Russian Jacques Bergier—mathematician, ex-spy, tireless student of the occult—said exactly the opposite of

5

political manuals: the world is made up of the most interesting things. There were alchemists, wizards, Cathars, Templars, and other words that meant it never had much success in the bookstores. A single copy was read by—at a minimum—ten people, given its exorbitant price. Anyway, Machu Picchu was in this book, and everyone wanted to go there, to Peru, and that's where you could find young people from all over the world (well, all over the world is a bit of an exaggeration, because those who lived in the Eastern Bloc didn't have the easiest time leaving their respective countries).

Anyway, getting back to our story: young people from all corners of the globe who had managed at least one priceless good known as a "passport" met up on the so-called hippie trails. No one knew exactly what the word "hippie" meant, and it didn't much matter. Perhaps it meant "a large tribe without a leader" or "delinquents who don't steal," or all the other descriptions we already covered earlier in this chapter.

Passports, these tiny little books issued by governments and placed along with cash (a lot or little, it doesn't really matter) inside a belt worn around the waist, served two purposes. The first, as we all know, was for crossing borders—as long as the border guards didn't get caught up in the news reports and decide to send someone back because they weren't accustomed to those clothes and that hair, or those flowers and those necklaces and those beads and those smiles belonging to people who seemed to live in a constant state of ecstasy—a state normally, though often unjustly, attributed to diabolical drugs that, according to the press, these young people consumed in ever greater quantities.

A passport's second purpose was to get its owner out of extreme situations where they'd run out of money and had nowhere to appeal for help. In such cases, the "Invisible Post" always provided much-needed information regarding locations where a passport might be sold. The price varied according to the country: a passport from Sweden, where everyone was blond, tall, and blue-eyed, wasn't worth much, since it could be resold only to those who were blond, tall, and blue-eyed, and so these were never the most sought-after. But a Brazilian passport was worth a fortune on the black market—the country was home not only to the blond, tall, and blue-eyed, but also to those who were tall and short, black people with dark eyes, Asians with narrow eyes, others of mixed race, Indians, Arabs, Jews; in other words, an enormous cultural melting pot that made a Brazilian passport one of the most coveted on the planet.

Once he'd sold this passport, the original owner would go to his country's consulate and, feigning horror and distress, explain that he'd been mugged and everything taken—he was completely out of money and had no passport. The consulates of wealthier countries would furnish a new passport and a free flight back to a traveler's country of origin, an offer immediately declined under the allegation that "somebody owes me a hefty sum, I need to get what's mine before I go." The poorer countries, often governed by harsh regimes in the hands of generals, would conduct a veritable interrogation to determine whether the applicant wasn't on a list of "terrorists" wanted for subversion. Once they'd verified that the young woman (or man) had a clean record, these countries were bound, against their will, to issue the new document. And they never offered a return flight, because they had no interest in having such derelicts influence generations that had been raised to respect God, family, and property.

Returning to the trails: after Machu Picchu, the next hot spot was Tiahuanaco, in Bolivia. Then Lhasa, in Tibet, where it was difficult to enter because, according to the "Invisible Post," there was a war between monks and Chinese soldiers. Of course it was difficult to imagine such a war, but everyone took it seriously and wasn't about to risk an endless trip to later end up a prisoner to the monks or the soldiers. The last of the era's great philosophers, who had just split up in April of that year, had a short time before proclaimed that the greatest wisdom on the planet was to be found in India. That was enough to send all the world's young people to the country in search of wisdom, knowledge, gurus, vows of poverty, enlightenment, and communion with My Sweet Lord.

The "Invisible Post," however, warned that Maharishi Mahesh Yogi, famed guru to the Beatles, had tried to engage in sexual relations with Mia Farrow. The actress had always been unhappy in love through the years. She had traveled to India at the invitation of the Beatles, possibly in the hope of finding a cure for this, which seemed to hound her like bad karma.

But everything suggests that Farrow's bad karma had accompanied her, John, Paul, George, and Ringo on their trip. According to Farrow, she was meditating in the great seer's cave when he grabbed her and tried to force her into sexual relations. By this point in the trip, Ringo had already returned to England because his wife hated Indian food and Paul had also decided to abandon the retreat, convinced that it wasn't doing anything for him. Only George and John remained in the Maharishi's temple when Mia came looking for them, in tears, and told them what had happened. The two immediately packed their bags, and when the Enlightened One came to ask what was going on, Lennon gave him a bruising response:

"You're the fucking Enlightened One, are you not? You ought to be able to figure it out."

Now, in September 1970, women ruled the world—or, more precisely, young hippie women ruled the world. Wherever they went, the men did so knowing these women weren't about to be seduced by the latest trends—the women knew much more about the subject than the men did. And so the men decided to accept once and for all that they needed these women; they constantly wore an expression of yearning, as though begging, "Please protect me, I'm all alone and I can't find anyone, I think the world's forgotten me and love has forsaken me forever." The women had their pick of men and never gave a thought to marriage, only to having a good time enjoying wild, intense sex. When it came to the important things, and even the most superficial and irrelevant, they had the last word. However, when the "Invisible Post" brought news of Mia Farrow's alleged sexual assault and Lennon's reaction, these women immediately decided to change their itineraries.

A new hippie trail was created, from Amsterdam (Holland) to Kathmandu (Nepal), on a bus that charged a fare of approximately a hundred dollars and traveled through countries that must have been pretty interesting: Turkey, Lebanon, Iran, Iraq, Afghanistan, Pakistan, and part of India (a great distance from the Maharishi's temple, it's worth noting). The trip lasted three weeks and an insane number of miles.

Karla was seated in Dam Square, asking herself when the guy who ought to accompany her on this magical adventure (in her mind, of course) would show up. She'd left a job behind in Rotterdam, just an hour's train ride away, but since she needed to save every last cent, she'd hitched a ride and the trip had taken almost a day. She had found out about the bus trip to Nepal in one of a dozen alternative newspapers published with the sweat, love, and effort of people who felt they had something to say to the world and subsequently sold for a nominal price.

After nearly a week of waiting, she was growing anxious. She'd approached a dozen young men from different countries who wanted nothing but to stay put, in that town square filled with nothing remarkable but a phallic monument, which at a minimum should have inspired virility and courage. But no; not a single one of them was inclined to travel to such unknown lands.

It wasn't a question of distance: most of them came from the

United States, Latin America, Australia, and other countries that required hefty prices for airline tickets, and they had faced many border checkpoints where they might have been barred and forced to return to their countries of origin before ever seeing one of the two world capitals. When they arrived there, they'd sit around the nondescript square, smoking marijuana and getting happy because there they could do so in plain view of the police, and they were soon literally kidnapped by the city's numerous sects and cults. They forgot, at least for a while, what they had heard their entire lives: *My boy, you have to go to college, get rid of this hair, don't bring shame to your parents, people (what people?) will say we didn't raise you right, whatever it is you're listening to, it isn't music, it's time you got a job,* or *Look at your brother (or sister), he's younger than you are and still manages to pay for his own fun without asking us for money.*

Far from their families' never-ending laments, they were now free people, Europe was a safe place (as long as they didn't get any ideas and cross the famous Iron Curtain to "invade" some Communist country), and they felt satisfied because our travels teach us everything we need to know for the rest of our lives, as long as there's no need to explain this to our parents.

"Dad, I know you want me to earn a diploma, but I can do that at any point in my life, what I need now are experiences."

There weren't any fathers who could make sense of this logic, and so the only thing left for their children to do was save some money, sell their things, and sneak out of the house while the rest of the family was sleeping.

Sure, Karla was surrounded by those who were free and determined to have experiences that most people lacked the courage to pursue. So why not go to Kathmandu by bus? Because it's not Europe, they replied. We don't have any idea what things are like over there. If something happens here, we can still go to the consulate and ask to be sent back to our countries (Karla hadn't heard of a single case where this had happened, but legend had it this was possible, and after much repetition legend becomes truth).

By the fifth day spent waiting for the man she'd choose as her "companion," she was growing desperate—she was spending money on a hostel when she could easily be sleeping on the Magic Bus (this was the official name of the bus that cost a hundred dollars and covered thousands of miles). She decided to go see a clairvoyant she'd been in the habit of visiting before going to Dam Square. The clairvoyant's place, as always, was empty—in September 1970, everyone either had paranormal capabilities or was in the process of developing them. But Karla was a practical woman, and though she meditated daily and was convinced she'd begun to open her third eye (an invisible spot in the middle of the forehead), up until then the men in her life had been all wrong for her, even when her intuition had assured her they were all right.

And so, she decided to appeal to the psychic, especially because her endless wait (nearly a week had already passed, an eternity!) was making her think she ought to travel on with a female companion. Though two women, on their own, crossing many countries could mean suicide; they would, at a minimum, be greeted with ugly looks and, in the worst case, if her grandmother were to be believed, they would end up being sold as "white slaves" (the term, for her, had an erotic sound but she didn't care to put her own flesh on the line to test it out).

The clairvoyant, whose name was Layla, was a little older than Karla. She wore clothes of white and the angelic smile of someone in contact with a Higher Being and welcomed Karla with a bow (Finally, someone to help me pay the day's rent, she must have thought to herself). She asked Karla to sit, which she did, and then the woman praised her for having chosen the energy center in the room. Karla pretended to herself that she'd truly managed to open her third eye, but her subconscious warned her that Layla must have said the same thing to everyone—or more precisely, to the few who entered that place.

At any rate, all this was irrelevant. Incense was burned ("This one is from Nepal," the clairvoyant told her, but Karla knew it had been manufactured nearby—incense was one of the hippies' major industries, along with necklaces, batik shirts, and patches with the peace sign or flowers or the phrase "Flower Power" to be sewn onto clothing). Layla grabbed a deck of cards and began to shuffle them, asked Karla to cut the deck, placed three cards on the table, and launched into the most conventional of interpretations. Karla interrupted her.

"I didn't come here for this. I only want to know if I'm going to find someone to go with me to the same place that you told me"—she placed great emphasis on the words *the same place that you told me*, because she didn't want to attract bad karma; if she'd said only *I want to go to the same place*, perhaps she would have ended up in some suburb of Amsterdam where the incense was actually made—"the same place you told me the incense came from."

Layla smiled, though her vibe had changed entirely—inside, she was burning with rage at having been interrupted at such a solemn moment.

"Yes, of course you will." It's the duty of every clairvoyant and tarot reader to tell her or his clients what they want to hear.

"When?"

"By end of the day tomorrow."

They were both taken by surprise.

For the first time, Karla felt the other woman was telling her the truth: her tone was positive, emphatic, as though her voice were coming from another dimension. Layla, for her part, was overcome with fear—it wasn't often things happened that way, and when they did she was afraid of being punished for entering that world which seemed both false and true without the proper reverence, though she justified her actions every night in her prayers, claiming that everything she was doing there on Earth was to help others to approach the things they wanted with greater positivity.

Karla immediately stood up from her energy center, paid for her half session, and left before the guy she was waiting for could arrive. "By end of the day tomorrow" was vague, it could well have meant that very same day. But whatever the case, she now knew she was waiting for someone.

She returned to her spot in Dam Square, opened the book

she had been reading, known then to only a few (which lent its author cult status): *The Lord of the Rings,* by J. R. R. Tolkien, a tale of mythic lands like those she intended to visit. She pretended not to hear the young men who every now and then came to bother her with some stupid question in a feeble attempt to begin a still feebler conversation.

Paulo and the man from Argentina had already discussed just about everything it was possible to discuss and now looked out on the flat terrain, but their minds were elsewhere—they both carried with them memories, names, curiosity, and above all a deep fear of what might happen when they reached the Dutch border, likely no further than twenty minutes away.

Paulo started to tuck his long hair inside his coat.

"You think you're going to fool the guards like that?" the Argentinean asked him. "There's nothing they haven't seen, absolutely nothing."

Paulo gave up. He asked his companion whether he wasn't worried.

"Of course I am. Especially because I already have two Dutch stamps on my passport, so they start to think I'm coming a bit too often. And this can mean only one thing."

Drug trafficking. But as far as Paulo knew, drugs were legal there.

"Of course not. They crack down hard on opioids. Same thing

for cocaine. Of course, there's no way for them to control LSD, all you have to do is dip the page of some book or a piece of cloth in the mixture and then cut it up and sell all the pieces. But everything they can detect can land you in prison."

Paulo thought it better to stop their conversation there. He was dying to know whether his fellow traveler was carrying something, but simply knowing would make him an accomplice. He had been in prison once before, although he had been totally innocent—in a country with the same decal on the doors of every airport: BRAZIL: LOVE IT OR LEAVE IT.

When we try to dismiss negative thoughts, it only attracts more diabolic energy, and for Paulo, the simple act of remembering what had happened in 1968 not only set his heart racing but had him reliving in excruciating detail that night at a restaurant in Ponta Grossa, in Paraná—a state in Brazil known for issuing passports to blond and blue-eyed men and women.

He was returning from his first lengthy trip along the latest hippie trail that was all the rage. With him was his girlfriend—eleven years his senior, born and raised under the Communist regime in Yugoslavia, the child of an aristocratic family that had lost everything but had given her an education that allowed her to learn four languages, flee to Brazil, and marry a millionaire. She would later divorce him when she found out he already considered her "old" at the age of thirty-three and had begun seeing a girl of seventeen. She then hired a top-notch lawyer who sued for enough damages that she would never have to work another day in her life.

Paulo and his girlfriend had set off together for Machu Picchu on the Death Train, a mode of transportation much different from the train car that he found himself in at that moment.

"Why do they call it the Death Train?" his girlfriend had asked the man responsible for checking tickets. "It's not as if we're traveling along any steep cliffs."

Paulo didn't have the least interest in the response, but he got one all the same.

"In the old days, these cars were used to transport lepers, the ill, and the bodies of the victims of a yellow fever epidemic that struck the region of Santa Cruz."

"I assume they've done an excellent job sanitizing the cars."

"We've had no casualties since, except for a miner or two forced to pull the pin and end it all."

The "miners" he referred to weren't those born in the mineral-rich region of Minas Gerais in Paulo's native Brazil but those who worked day and night in the tin mines of Bolivia. Well, it was a civilized world they were living in; he hoped no one would decide to pull any pins that day. To the relief of both, the majority of the travelers were women with their bowler hats and colorful dress.

They arrived in La Paz, the country's capital, 12,000 feet above sea level, but, having made the ascent by train, they barely felt the effects of the thin air. Even so, when they stepped off the train, they saw a young man wearing clothes that identified his tribe sitting on the ground, a bit disoriented. They asked him what was wrong ("I can't breathe"). A man who was passing by advised that he try chewing coca leaves, which could be easily found at any of the nearby street markets. This was a tribal custom that helped those who lived there to face the high altitudes. The young man soon felt better and asked them to leave him where they had found him—he was to go to Machu Picchu that very day.

The receptionist at the hotel they'd chosen called Paulo's girlfriend to the side, said a few words, and then completed their registration. They went up to their room and immediately fell asleep, but not before Paulo asked what the receptionist had said.

"No sex for the first two days."

It was easy to understand why. He was in no condition to do anything.

They spent two days in the Bolivian capital without sex, without suffering any collateral effects of the *soroche,* as the lack of oxygen was called. Both he and his girlfriend attributed this to the therapeutic effects of the coca leaves, which in reality had nothing to do with it; *soroche* occurs only in those who depart from sea level and quickly climb to great heights—in other words, by plane—without allowing their bodies the time to adjust. The couple had spent seven long days on the Death Train. Much more ideal for adjusting to their environs and much safer than air travel—in the airport at Santa Cruz de la Sierra, Paulo had seen a monument honoring the "heroic pilots who laid down their lives in the line of duty."

In La Paz, they came across their first hippies—who, as a global tribe conscious of the responsibility and solidarity they owed one another, always wore the famous symbol of the inverted Viking rune. In Bolivia, a country where everyone sported colorful ponchos, jackets, shirts, and suits, it was practically impossible to know who was who without the help of the rune sewn onto jackets or pant legs.

These first hippies they came across were two Germans and a Canadian woman. Paulo's girlfriend, who spoke German, was soon invited for a walk through the city, while he and the Canadian woman looked at each other, unsure exactly what to say. When, half an hour later, the three others returned from their walk, they all decided they ought to depart immediately rather than spend their money there: they would continue on to the highest freshwater lake in the world, navigate its waters by boat, get off at the other end—which would already put them in Peruvian territory—and head straight for Machu Picchu.

Everything would have gone according to plan if, when they arrived at the shores of Titicaca (the highest navigable freshwater lake in the world), the group hadn't found themselves before an ancient monument known as the Gate of the Sun. Gathered around the monument were still more hippies, holding hands in a ritual that they were afraid to interrupt but, at the same time, would also have liked to be a part of.

A young woman caught sight of them, silently beckoned them with a nod, and all five of them were able to sit with the others.

It wasn't necessary to explain why they were there; the gate spoke for itself. There was a crack straight down the middle of the upper part of the stone, possibly caused by a lightning strike, but the rest was a true wonder of low reliefs, a guardian of stories from a time already forgotten and yet still present, wishing to be remembered and discovered anew. It was sculpted from a single stone, and across the upper part were angels, the gods, lost symbols of a culture that, according to the locals, would show the way to recover the world in the event it was destroyed by human greed. Paulo, who could see through the opening in the gate onto Lake Titicaca in the distance, began to cry, as though he were in contact with those who had built that structure— people who had abandoned the area in a hurry, before they'd even had a chance to finish their work, fearful that something or someone would appear, demanding that they stop. The young woman who had called them to the circle smiled, she too with tears in her eyes. The rest stood with eyes closed, speaking to the ancestors, seeking to discover what had brought them all there, respecting this great mystery.

Those who wish to learn magic ought to begin by looking around them. All that God wished to reveal to man He placed right in front of him, the so-called Tradition of the Sun.

The Tradition of the Sun belongs to all—it wasn't made for the erudite or the pure but for everyday people. Energy is to be found in the tiniest things man encounters in his path; the world is the true classroom, the Love Supreme knows you are alive and will teach you all you need to know.

Everyone was silent, paying close attention to something they could not quite understand but which they knew to be true. One of the young women there sang a song in a language Paulo could not understand. A young man—perhaps the oldest among them—stood up, opened his arms, and said a prayer:

> *May God give you . . .*
> *For every storm, a rainbow,*
> *For every tear, a smile,*
> *For every care, a promise,*
> *And a blessing in each trial.*
> *For every problem life sends,*

A faithful friend to share,
For every sigh, a sweet song,
And an answer for each prayer.

At this exact moment, a horn sounded from a boat, which was in fact a ship built in England, disassembled, and transported to a city in Chile, then carried piece by piece on the backs of mules to an altitude of 12,000 feet, where the lake was to be found.

Everyone climbed on board, off toward the ancient lost city of the Incas.

The days they spent there were unforgettable—rarely did someone actually manage to reach that place, only those who were God's children, the free of spirit ready to face the unknown without fear.

They slept in abandoned houses without roofs, gazing at the stars; they made love; they ate the food they'd brought. Each day they bathed completely nude in the river that ran below the mountain, and discussed the possibility that the gods had actually been astronauts and landed on Earth in that region of the world. They had all read the same book by a Swiss author who often interpreted the Incan drawings as trying to depict celestial travelers; just as they'd read Lobsang Rampa, the Tibetan monk who spoke of opening one's third eye—until one day an Englishman told everyone sitting there on the central square in Machu Picchu that the so-called monk was named Cyril Henry Hoskin and was a plumber from the English countryside whose identity had recently been discovered and whose credentials had already been refuted by the Dalai Lama.

The entire group was filled with disappointment, above

all because, like Paulo, they were convinced that there truly did exist something between their eyes, called a pineal gland, though its usefulness had not yet been discovered by scientists. And so, the third eye did exist—though not in the way Lobsang Cyril Rampa Hoskin had described it.

On the third morning, Paulo's girlfriend decided to return home, and she also decided—without leaving any room for doubt—that Paulo ought to accompany her. Without saying goodbye to anyone or looking back, they left before sunrise and spent two days descending the eastern face of the mountain range in a bus full of people, domestic animals, food, and folk crafts. Paulo took the opportunity to buy a colorful bag, which he was able to fold and stash inside his backpack. He also decided that he would never again embark on a bus trip that lasted longer than a day.

From Lima they hitchhiked to Santiago de Chile—the world was a safe place, cars stopped, though the drivers were a bit fearful of the couple on account of their clothing. In Santiago, after a good night's sleep, they asked somebody to draw a map showing them how to go back across the Andes through a tunnel that connected the country to Argentina. They continued on toward Brazil—again hitching a ride because Paulo's girlfriend kept repeating that the money they still had might be necessary in case of some medical emergency—she was always prudent, always the elder, always a product of a practical Communist upbringing that never allowed her to relax entirely.

In Brazil, having reached a part of the country where the majority of those with passports were blond and blue-eyed, they decided to stop again, at his girlfriend's suggestion.

"Let's go see Vila Velha. They say the place is incredible."

They didn't foresee the nightmare.

They had no sense of the hell to come.

They weren't prepared for what awaited them.

They had been to several incredible, unique places with something about them that suggested that in the future they would be destroyed by hordes of tourists who thought only of acquiring and amassing amenities for their own homes. But the way Paulo's girlfriend spoke left no room for doubt, there was no question mark at the end of her sentence, she was merely notifying him of what they would do.

Yes, of course, let's go to Vila Velha. An incredible place. A geological site with remarkable natural sculptures shaped by the wind—which the nearest city tried to promote at all costs, spending a fortune in the process. Everyone knew of Vila Velha's existence, but the less informed would drive on past to a beach in a state bordering Rio de Janeiro. Others were curious but thought it too much work to make the journey.

Paulo and his girlfriend were the only visitors there, and they marveled at the way nature manages to create floral calyxes, turtles, camels—or rather, the way we manage to give names to everything, even if the camel in question really looked like a pomegranate to the woman and an orange to him. At any rate, unlike everything they'd seen at Tiahuanaco, these sandstone sculptures were open to all sorts of interpretations.

From there, they grabbed a ride to the closest city. Paulo's girlfriend, knowing it wouldn't be long before they arrived home, decided—it was she, in fact, who decided everything—that they would, that night, for the first time in many weeks, sleep in a nice hotel and have meat for dinner! Meat, one of the things they did best in that region of Brazil, something they hadn't tasted since they'd left La Paz—the price always seemed exorbitant.

They registered at a genuine hotel, took a bath, made love, and walked down to the lobby, thinking they would ask for a recommendation of a rodizio restaurant, where they could eat as much as they wanted, buffet-style.

While they waited for the concierge to appear, two men approached and, dispensing with pleasantries, ordered Paulo and his girlfriend to follow them outside. Both had their hands in their pockets, as though they held guns, and wished to make this quite clear.

"Don't be crazy," Paulo's girlfriend said, convinced they were being held up. "I have a diamond ring up in the room."

But the two men had already taken them by the arm and pushed them outside—immediately separating them from one another. On the deserted street were two cars without any sort of identification, and two other men—one of them pointing a gun at the couple.

"Don't move, and don't do anything suspicious. We're going to search you."

The brutes began to pat them down. Paulo's girlfriend still tried to protest, but he had already entered a sort of trance, completely dazed. The only thing he managed to do was look around to see if some witness would end up calling the police.

"Shut your mouth, you stupid slut," one of the men said. They took the couple's belts containing their passports and money, and each of the two was forced into the backseat of one of the parked cars. Paulo didn't so much as have time to see what was happening to his girlfriend—nor did she know what was happening to him.

Inside the car was another man.

"Put this on," he said, handing Paulo a hood. "And lie down on the floor."

Paulo did exactly as he was told. His brain was no longer

processing anything. The car sped away. He would have liked to tell these men that his family had money, that he would pay any ransom, but the words would not leave his mouth.

The train's pace began to slow, a likely sign they were approaching the Dutch border.

"Is everything all right with you, dude?" the Argentinean asked.

Paulo nodded, searching for something to talk about, to exorcise his negative thoughts. It had been over a year since the incident at Vila Velha, and most of the time he managed to control the demons inside his head. But whenever the word POLICE entered his line of sight, even if it were just a customs official, his terror returned. Only this time when the terror returned so did the entire story, which he'd already told a few friends, though always maintaining a certain distance, as though observing himself from afar. However, this time—and for the very first time—he was repeating the story to himself alone.

"If they bar us at the border, no problem. We can go to Belgium and cross somewhere else," the Argentinean suggested.

Paulo wasn't in much of a mood to talk to this character—his paranoia had returned. What if the man really was trafficking hard drugs? What if they decided Paulo was an accomplice and threw him in prison until he could prove his innocence?

The train came to a stop. It wasn't customs but a tiny station in the middle of nowhere where two people got on and five got off. The Argentinean, seeing that Paulo wasn't in much of a talking mood, decided to leave him alone with his thoughts, but he was worried—Paulo's expression had changed entirely. He asked one last time:

"So, everything really is all right with you, right?"

"I'm performing an exorcism."

The Argentinean got the message and said nothing more.

Paulo knew that there, in Europe, the things he'd been through did not happen. Or, rather, they had happened but in the past. He always asked himself how those walking to the gas chambers in the concentration camps or lined up for death at a mass grave, watching the firing squad execute the front line, never had the slightest reaction, never tried to run, never attacked their executioners.

The answer was simple: their panic was so great that they were no longer present. The brain blocks out everything, there's neither terror nor fear, just a strange submission to what's about to occur. Emotions vanish to make way for a sort of limbo, where everything happens in a zone that scientists have been unable to explain to this day. Doctors have a label for this, "temporary stress-induced schizophrenia," and have never bothered looking into the exact consequences of the flat affect, as they call it.

And, perhaps to expel the ghosts of his past once and for all, Paulo relived the entire ordeal through to the very end.

The man in the backseat with him seemed a bit more humane than the others who had approached them at the hotel.

"Don't worry, we're not going to kill you. Lie down on the floor."

Paulo wasn't worried—his head was no longer processing anything. It was like he had entered an alternate reality; his brain refused to accept what was happening to him. The only thing he did was ask:

"Can I hold on to your leg?"

"Of course," the man responded.

Paulo clutched the man's leg, perhaps his grip was stronger than he thought, perhaps he was hurting the man, but the other man didn't move. He allowed Paulo to continue—he knew what Paulo was going through, and he likely took no pleasure in watching such a young man, full of life, endure that experience. But he also followed orders.

———

Paulo couldn't say exactly how long the drive lasted, and the longer they drove, the more he became convinced he was about to be executed. He had already managed to make some sense of what was going on—he had been captured by paramilitary officers and was officially disappeared. But what did that matter now?

The car came to a stop. They tore him from the backseat and lugged him down what seemed like a hallway. Suddenly his foot hit something on the floor, a sort of metal strip.

"Please, could we go slower?" he asked.

That's when he received the first blow across his head.

"Shut your mouth, terrorist!"

He fell to the ground. They ordered him to stand up and remove all his clothing—carefully, to ensure the hood stayed in place. He did what he was told. They immediately began to beat him, and because he didn't know where each blow was coming from, his body could no longer prepare itself and his muscles were unable to contract, resulting in pain far worse than anything he'd ever experienced in his childhood scuffles. He fell again, and now each punch was replaced by a kick. The beating lasted ten or fifteen minutes, until a voice ordered the men to stop.

He was still conscious, but he wasn't sure if he had broken something; he couldn't move he was in so much pain. Despite this, the voice that had ordered an end to that first torture session ordered him back to his feet. The voice began to ask a series of questions about the guerrilla movement, about comrades, about what he'd been doing in Bolivia, whether he was in touch with Che Guevara and his gang, where the weapons were hidden. He threatened to gouge Paulo's eye out as soon as he could confirm his involvement. Another voice, this one from the "good cop," took a different tack. It was better to confess to the robbery they'd committed at a nearby bank—that way, everything would be cleared up; Paulo would be put in prison for his crimes but they wouldn't touch him again.

That was the moment, as he struggled to his feet, that he began to emerge from the lethargic state he found himself in and regained something he had always considered one of man's greatest attributes: the survival instinct. He needed a way out of that situation. He needed to tell them he was innocent.

They ordered him to tell them everything he'd done in the previous week. Paulo recounted everything in detail, though he knew they'd never heard of Machu Picchu.

"Don't waste your time trying to fool us," the "bad cop" said. "We found the map in your hotel room. You and Blondie were spotted at the scene of the crime."

Map?

The man showed him a piece of paper through the opening in his hood, a drawing someone in Chile had given them showing the way to the tunnel that crossed the Andes.

"The Communists think they're going to win the next elections. That Allende will use Moscow's gold to corrupt all of Latin America. But you'd be wrong. What's your role in the alliance they're forming? Who are your contacts in Brazil?"

Paulo begged them, he swore none of that was true, he was just some guy who wanted to travel and see the world—at the same time he asked them what they were doing with his girlfriend.

"The one sent from that Communist country, Yugoslavia,

to put an end to democracy in Brazil? She's getting what she deserves" came the bad cop's response.

His paralyzing fear threatened to return, but Paulo needed to keep himself under control. He needed to discover how to escape this nightmare. He needed to wake up.

Someone placed a box with some wires and a crank between his feet. Another person told him they called it a telephone—they only needed to tape the metal clamps to his body and crank the handle and Paulo would get "a shock no man could handle."

Suddenly, seeing the machine before him, he hit upon his only way out of there. He abandoned his submissive posture and raised his voice:

"You think I'm afraid of a little shock? You think I'm afraid of a little pain? Well, don't you worry—I'll torture myself. I've already been to the nuthouse not one, not two, but three times; I've had all sorts of electric shocks, I can do the job for you. But this isn't news to you, I'll bet you know everything about my life."

When he'd finished, he began to dig his nails into his flesh and draw blood, tear skin, screaming the entire time that they knew everything, that they could kill him, he didn't care, he believed in reincarnation, he would come back for them. Them and their families, as soon as he made it to the other world.

Someone came and restrained him. Everyone seemed horrified at what he was doing, though no one said anything.

"Stop this, Paulo," the "good cop" said. "Can you explain the map to me?"

Paulo spoke in the voice of someone who was having a psychotic episode. He screamed as he explained what had happened in Santiago—they needed directions to the tunnel that connected Chile and Argentina.

"My girlfriend, where's my girlfriend?"

His screams grew louder and louder, in the hope that she could hear him. The "good cop" tried to calm him down—by the looks of it, at that time, the very beginning of the so-called Years of Lead, the agents of repression hadn't yet reached their peak brutality.

The man asked him to stop shaking. If he was innocent there was no reason to worry, but first they needed to verify everything he'd told them—he would have to remain there a little while longer. The man didn't say how long, but he offered Paulo a cigarette. Paulo noticed that the others had begun leaving the room, they weren't interested in him anymore.

"Wait for me to leave. When you hear the sound of the door closing, you can take off your hood. Every time someone comes and knocks on the door, put it back on. As soon as we have all the information we need, you can leave."

"What about my girlfriend?" Paulo screamed again.

He didn't deserve this. No matter how bad a son he had been, no matter how many headaches he'd given his parents, he didn't deserve this. He was innocent—but, if he'd had a gun, he was capable of shooting all of them then and there. There's nothing worse than the feeling of being punished for something you haven't done.

"Don't worry. We're not some monster rapists. We only want to put an end to those who want to put an end to our country."

The man left, the door clicked shut, and Paulo removed his hood. He was in a soundproof room, one outfitted with a metal doorsill. That's what he'd tripped over on his way in. There was an enormous one-way mirror to his right—it must have served to monitor whoever was being held there. There were two or three bullet holes in the ceiling, and one of them looked to have a strand of hair coming out of it. But he needed to pretend none of this interested him. He looked at his body, at the scabs forming from the blood that he had shed; he ran his hands over his entire body and saw that nothing was broken—they were masters at leaving no permanent traces, and perhaps that was why his reaction had alarmed them.

He imagined that the next step would be to call Rio de Janeiro and confirm his stories about the mental institution, the electric shock therapy, each step he and his girlfriend had taken—her foreign passport might either protect her or spell her demise, seeing as how she came from a Communist country.

If he were lying, he would be tortured nonstop for days on end. If he were speaking the truth, perhaps they would reach the conclusion that he really was just some drugged-up hippie from a rich family and let him go.

He wasn't lying, and he hoped they wouldn't take long to discover this.

He wasn't sure how long he'd been there—there were no windows, the light never went out, and the only face he'd been able to catch a glimpse of was that of the torture site's photographer. Were those barracks? A police station? The photographer ordered him to remove his hood, placed the camera in front of his face in such a way to conceal that he was nude, ordered him to stand profile, took another photo, and left without exchanging a single word.

Even the knocks on his door defied any schedule that might allow him to ascertain a routine—at times, lunch was served only a short time after breakfast, and the hours often dragged until dinner arrived. When he needed to go to the bathroom, he'd knock on the door, replacing the hood, until, mostly likely through the one-way mirror, they figured out what he wanted. At times he would try to speak with the figure who led him to the bathroom, but he received no response. Only silence.

He spent most of his time sleeping. One day (or night?) he tried to make use of the experience to meditate or concentrate on some higher being—he recalled that San Juan de la Cruz had spoken of the dark night of the soul, that monks spent years in desert caves or high up in the Himalayas. He could follow their example, use what was happening to try to transform himself into a better person. He had worked out that it had been the hotel doorman—he and his girlfriend had been the only guests—who had reported the couple. At times, he felt like going back and killing the man as soon as he was free, and at others, he felt that the best way to serve God would be to forgive the man from the bottom of his heart because he knew not what he was doing.

But forgiveness is a delicate art. Throughout all of his travels he'd sought to be one with the universe. But this didn't include, at least not at that moment in his life, putting up with those who always laughed at his long hair, stopped in the street to ask how long it had been since he'd had a shower, told him that his bright-colored clothes showed he wasn't secure in his own sexuality, asked how many men he'd slept with, told him to quit being a bum, stop the drugs, and find a decent job, to do his part to lift the country out of its economic crisis.

His hatred of injustice, the desire for revenge, and the lack of forgiveness didn't allow him to focus as he should have, and soon his meditation was interrupted by sordid thoughts—sordid but justified, the way he saw it. Had they told his family?

His parents hadn't known when he planned to return, but they wouldn't have thought anything of his prolonged absence. Both his father and mother always blamed it on the fact that he had a girlfriend eleven years his senior, who sought to use him to fulfill unspeakable desires, to break the routine of a frustrated socialite and foreigner in the wrong country. She was a manipulator of young men who needed a mother figure. Paulo was not like all his friends, like all his enemies, like everyone else in the world who lived their lives without causing problems for anyone, without forcing their families to explain their sons' lives, without being looked at like *those people* who hadn't raised their children right. Paulo's sister was studying chemical engineering and distinguishing herself as a top student, but their pride in her was not enough, for his parents were much more worried about returning him to the world they knew.

Anyway, after some time, it was impossible to say how much, Paulo began to think he deserved everything that was happening to him. Some of his friends had joined the armed resistance knowing what awaited them, and only he had paid the consequences—his punishment must have come from the heavens, not men. For all the distress he'd caused, he deserved to be naked on the floor of a cell with three bullet holes (he'd counted), looking deep inside himself and finding no strength, no spiritual consolation, no voice like the one that spoke to him at the Gate of the Sun.

All he did was sleep. Always thinking he would wake up from the nightmare and always opening his eyes in the same place, on the same floor. Always thinking that the worst was over, and always waking up in a sweat, racked with fear, each time he heard a knock on the door—perhaps they hadn't been able to confirm anything he said and the torture would resume, even more violent than before.

S omeone knocked on the door—Paulo had just finished his dinner, but he knew they might well serve him breakfast to increase his sense of disorientation. He put on his hood, heard the sound of the door opening and someone throwing things across the floor.

"Get dressed. Careful not to remove your hood."

It was the voice of the "good cop," or the "good torturer," as he preferred to refer to him privately. The man stood there while Paulo got dressed and put on his shoes. When he'd finished, the man grabbed him by the arm, asked him to be careful with the metal bar at the door (where he'd already passed many times on his way to the bathroom, but perhaps this man had felt the need to say some kind words), and reminded him that his only scars were those he'd inflicted himself.

They walked for about three minutes, and then another voice spoke: "The Variant is waiting for you outside."

Variant? Later he realized it was a type of car, but at that moment he thought it was some sort of code, something like "the firing squad is ready and waiting."

They led him to the car and handed him some paper and a pen that he could just make out from beneath his hood. He didn't even think about reading it, he'd sign whatever they wanted, his confession would at least put an end to his maddening isolation. But the "good torturer" explained that it was a list of his belongings found in the hotel. The backpacks were in the trunk.

The backpacks! He had said "backpacks," plural. But Paulo was in such a daze that he didn't even notice.

He did as he was told. A door opened on the other side of the car. Through the opening in his hood, Paulo caught a glimpse of familiar clothing—it was her! They ordered her to do the same thing, to sign a document, but she refused, saying she had to read what was written first. Her tone of voice made it clear she hadn't panicked through the entire ordeal; she was in full control of her emotions, and the figure waited obediently as she read. When she finished, she finally signed the piece of paper and then placed her hand on Paulo's.

"No physical contact," the "good torturer" said.

She ignored him, and for a second, Paulo thought they would both be taken inside again and beaten for disobeying. He tried removing his hand, but she tightened her grip and held it there.

The "good torturer" simply closed the door and ordered the car forward. Paulo asked her whether she was all right, and she responded by railing against everything that had happened. Someone gave a chuckle in the front seat, and Paulo asked her to *please* quiet down, they could discuss it all later, or another day, or wherever it was they were being taken—perhaps a real prison.

"No one makes you sign a document saying our things have been returned to us if they have no intention of letting us out," she told him. The figure in the front seat laughed again—actually, there were two people laughing. The driver was not alone.

"I've always heard that women are more courageous and more intelligent than men," one of them said. "We've noticed this here among the prisoners."

This time, it was the passenger who asked his companion to quiet down. The car sped on for a while longer, stopped, and the man on the driver's side asked them to remove their hoods.

It was one of the men who had nabbed the couple at the hotel, he was of Asian descent—this time, he was smiling. He climbed out with them, went to the trunk, grabbed their backpacks, and handed them over instead of throwing them on the ground.

"You can go now. Take a left at the next light, walk about twenty minutes, and you'll be at the bus station."

He got back in the car and slowly pulled away, as though he didn't have a care about everything that had just taken place. That was the way things were now in Brazil, he was in control, and there was nothing anyone could do about it.

Paulo glanced over at his girlfriend, who glanced back. They embraced and held their kiss for some time and then continued on to the bus station. It was dangerous to stay there, he thought. His girlfriend didn't seem to have changed a bit, as though all those days—weeks, months, years?—had merely been a short pause in the trip of their dreams, as though the positive memories were what remained and could not be overshadowed by what had happened. He picked up the pace, avoiding any suggestion that everything was her fault, that they never should have stopped to see the sculptures molded by the wind, that if they had kept moving, none of those things would have happened—though it wasn't anybody's fault, not his girlfriend's, not Paulo's, not that of anyone they knew.

He was being ridiculous and weak. Suddenly he felt a terrible headache, so intense he almost couldn't walk any further, flee back to the city where he'd grown up, or return to the Gate of the Sun and ask the ancient and forgotten inhabitants there what had happened. He propped himself up against a wall and let the backpack slide to the ground.

"You know what that is?" his girlfriend asked—and then quickly gave the answer. "I know the answer because I've already been through the same thing when my country was being bombed. The whole time, it was like my brain slowed down, the blood didn't flow to my arteries the way it did before. It'll pass in two or three hours, but we'll buy some aspirin at the bus station."

She grabbed his backpack, lifted him with her shoulder, and dragged him forward—slowly, at first, then gradually gaining speed.

Oh, woman, what a woman. A shame that when he suggested they set off together for the two centers of the world—Piccadilly Circus and Dam Square—she told him she was tired of traveling and, to be honest, she no longer loved him. They ought to go their separate ways.

The train stopped, and the dreaded sign written in several languages came into view: BORDER CONTROL.

Some officers boarded and began to walk the aisles. Paulo was calmer now, the exorcism was over, but he couldn't get a verse from the Bible, more precisely from the Book of Job, out of his head: "What I feared has come upon me."

He needed to remain in control—anyone is capable of sniffing out fear.

Whatever. If, as the Argentinean said, the worst thing that could happen would be their getting turned away, there was no problem. There were other borders they could cross. And if somehow they didn't manage, there was always the other center of the world—Piccadilly Circus.

Paulo was overcome with a deep sense of calm after reliving the terror he'd experienced a year and a half earlier. As though everything truly had to be faced without fear, as a mere fact of life—we don't choose the things that happen to us, but we can choose how we react to them.

He realized that up until that moment the cancer of injustice, of despair, and of powerlessness had begun spreading throughout his entire astral body, but now he was free.

He was beginning anew.

The border agents entered the cabin where Paulo and the Argentinean sat with four other people they didn't know. As expected, the guards ordered the two of them to step off the train. Outside, there was a chill in the air, though night had only just begun to fall.

But nature follows a cycle that's repeated in the human soul: a plant gives birth to the flower so that the bees might come and create the fruit. The fruit produces seeds, which transform once again into plants, which again bloom with flowers, which attract the bees, which fertilize the plant and cause it to produce yet more fruit, and so on and so forth until the end of eternity. Greetings, autumn, time to leave behind all that is old, the terrors of the past, and make way for the new.

Some of the young men and women were led inside the customs station. No one said a thing, and Paulo made sure to stay as far away as possible from the Argentinean—who took note and did not seek to burden him with his presence or his conversation. Perhaps he understood at that moment that he was being judged, that the young man from Brazil must have had his suspicions, but he'd seen Paulo's face as it was covered by a dark shadow, and now it was full of light once again—perhaps "full of light" was an exaggeration, but at the very least the intense sadness of only moments before had disappeared.

———

They began calling each person individually to a room—and no one knew what was said inside because they exited through another door. Paulo was the third to be summoned.

Seated behind a desk was a uniformed guard who asked for Paulo's passport and leafed through a large file full of names.

"One of my dreams is to go . . ." Paulo began, but he was immediately warned not to interrupt the official as he worked.

His heartbeat quickened, and Paulo was battling against himself, to believe that autumn had arrived, dead leaves had begun to fall, a new man had been born from the individual who until then had been in absolute tatters.

Bad vibrations only attract more bad vibrations, so he tried to calm himself down, particularly after he noticed the guard was wearing an earring in one ear, something unthinkable in any of the other countries he'd visited. He sought to distract himself with the room full of documents, a photo of the queen, and a poster of a windmill. The figure before him quickly set the list aside and didn't even bother asking what Paulo was going to do in Holland—the guard only wanted to know if he had enough money for the trip back to his country.

Paulo confirmed he did—he had learned that this was the main condition for travel to any foreign country and had bought an outrageously expensive round-trip ticket arriving first in Rome, even though the return date was a year out. He reached for the belt that stayed hidden around his waist, ready to provide proof for what he'd said, but the guard told him it wasn't necessary, he wanted to know how much money he had.

"Around sixteen hundred dollars. A little more, perhaps, but I'm not sure how much I spent on the train."

He'd stepped off the plane in Europe with seventeen hundred dollars, his earnings as a college entrance exam instructor at the theater school he had himself attended. The Rome ticket had been the cheapest he could find; when he arrived there he'd discovered via the "Invisible Post" that there the hippies often gathered in the Piazza di Spagna, at the foot of the Spanish Steps. He'd found a place to sleep in a park, lived off sandwiches and ice cream, and could have stayed in Rome—where he'd met a Spanish woman from Galicia who immediately became a friend and shortly thereafter his girlfriend. He had finally bought the bestseller of his generation, which he had no doubt was about to make all the difference in his life: *Europe on 5 Dollars a Day.* During the days he'd spent on the Piazza di Spagna, he'd noticed that it wasn't only the hippies who used the book— which listed the cheapest hotels and restaurants, plus important tourist attractions in each city—but more conventional travelers, too, known as "squares."

He would have no trouble getting around when he arrived in Amsterdam. He had decided to continue on toward his first destination (the second was Piccadilly Circus, as he never tired of remembering) when the Spanish woman told him she was going to Athens, in Greece.

Once again he reached for his money, but he quickly received his stamped passport back. The agent asked whether he was carrying any fruits or vegetables—he was carrying two apples, and the guard asked him to throw them in a trash bin just outside the station as soon as he left.

"And how do I get to Amsterdam from here?"

He was informed he would need to take a local train, which passed by every half hour—the ticket he'd bought in Rome was good to his final destination.

The agent directed him to the exit, and Paulo once again found himself out in the fresh air, waiting on the next train, surprised and pleased that they had taken him at his word when it came to his ticket and the money he was carrying.

Truly, he was in another world.

Karla didn't waste an entire afternoon sitting around in Dam Square, particularly because it had begun to rain and the psychic had assured her that the person she was waiting for would arrive the following day. She'd decided to go to the movies to watch *2001: A Space Odyssey,* which everyone had told her was a masterpiece, despite the fact she didn't have much interest in science fiction films.

Alas, it truly was a masterpiece. The film had helped her kill some time while she waited, and the ending showed her something she thought she knew—but in reality it wasn't a question of what she thought or didn't think, it was an absolute and indisputable fact: time is circular and always returns to the same spot. We are born from a seed, we grow, we age, we die, we return to the earth and again become the seed that, sooner or later, becomes reincarnate in another person. Though her family was Lutheran, she had flirted for a time with Catholicism, and during the Mass she had begun to attend regularly, she would recite all the professions of faith. This was the line she liked the most: *"I believe [. . .] in the resurrection of the body and life everlasting. Amen."*

The resurrection of the body—she had tried once to speak to a priest about that passage, asking him about reincarnation, but the clergyman told her it wasn't about that at all. She asked him what it was about. His response—as stupid as they come—was that she didn't yet have the maturity to understand. At that moment she began to slowly drift away from Catholicism because she'd noticed that the priest had no idea what the passage was about either.

"Amen," she repeated that day as she made her way back to her hotel. She kept her ears open for anything, in case God decided to speak to her. After distancing herself from the Church, she decided to seek out—via Hinduism, Taoism, Buddhism, African religions, the various forms of yoga—some sort of response to her questions about the meaning of life. A poet had said many centuries before: "Your light fills the entire Universe / The lamp of love burns and rescues Understanding."

Because love had always been such a complicated thing throughout her life, so complicated that she constantly avoided thinking about it, she arrived at the conclusion that this Understanding was within herself—that was, after all, what the founders of each of these religions had preached. And now that everything she saw reminded her of the Lord, she sought to make each of her actions a gesture of thanks for her life.

That was enough. The worst killing is that which kills the joy we get from life.

———

She stopped in a coffee shop, where there were several varieties of marijuana and hashish for sale. But the only thing she did was drink a coffee and trade a few words with another young woman, also Dutch, who seemed out of place and was also there having a coffee. Wilma was her name. They decided they would go to the Paradiso but they soon changed their minds, perhaps because the place was no longer a novelty for anyone, just as the drugs sold there weren't either. A great thing for tourists but boring for those who had always had them within reach.

One day—one day in a far-off future—governments around the world would conclude that the best way to put an end to all they considered a "problem" was to legalize it. A great deal of hashish's mystique was its being illegal and, as a result, highly sought after.

"But that's in nobody's interest," Wilma said when Karla shared her thoughts. "They earn billions of dollars by cracking down. They consider themselves above the rest. Crusaders for society and the family. An excellent political platform—putting an end to drugs. What other idea would they replace it with? Sure, an end to poverty, but no one believes in that anymore."

Their conversation came to an end and they sat staring at their coffee cups. Karla thought back to the movie, to *The Lord of the Rings,* to her life. She had never really had any interesting experiences. She had been born into a pious family, had studied at a Lutheran high school, knew the Bible by heart, had lost her virginity as an adolescent with a Dutch boy who was also a virgin at the time, had traveled some through Europe, had found a job when she turned twenty (by this time she was twenty-three). The days seemed to stretch on, to repeat themselves, she became

Catholic merely to rebel against her family, decided to leave her parents' house and live alone, had a series of boyfriends who came into and out of her life and her body for periods varying from two days to two months. She thought that the blame for all of that belonged to Rotterdam and its cranes, its gray streets, and its harbor, where stories were constantly coming in that were much more interesting than those she typically heard from her friends.

She got along better with foreigners. The only time her routine of absolute freedom was interrupted was when she decided to fall hopelessly in love with a Frenchman ten years her senior. She convinced herself that she could make that all-consuming love mutual—though she knew quite well that the Frenchman was only interested in sex, a discipline she excelled in and was always striving to improve. After a short while she left the Frenchman in Paris, having come to the conclusion that she hadn't truly discovered the purpose of love in her life. This was a condition of her own making—all the people she knew had at one moment or another begun to talk about the importance of marriage, children, cooking, having someone to watch television with, take to the theater, travel the world with, bring back little surprises each time they came back home, get pregnant, raise the children, pretend they never saw each of their husband's or wife's petty betrayals, say that their children were their only purpose in life, worry about what to have for dinner, what they would grow up to be like, how things were going at school, at work, in life.

In this way, they extended for a few more years their sense of usefulness on this earth, until sooner or later all the children left—the house became empty, and the only things that mattered at all were Sunday lunches, the whole family together again, always pretending everything was perfect, always pretending there were no petty jealousies or competition between them, while they all hurled invisible daggers through the air: because I make more than you do, my wife is an architect, we just bought a house like you'd never believe, that sort of thing.

Two years earlier she'd figured out that it didn't make sense to go on living this absolute freedom. She began to think about death, flirted with the idea of entering a convent, she even went to the place where the Discalced Carmelites lived entirely cut off from the world. She told them she had been baptized, discovered Christ, and wanted to be his bride for the rest of her life. The mother superior asked her to think it over for a month before making her final decision—and during this month she had time to imagine herself in a cell, forced to pray from dawn to dusk, repeating the same words over and over until they lost meaning, and she discovered she was unable to lead a life whose routine might well drive her insane. The mother superior had been right—she never went back; no matter how bad the routine of absolute freedom was, she could always discover new and interesting things to do.

A sailor from Bombay, in addition to being an excellent lover (something she rarely encountered), led her to discover Eastern mysticism. It was then that she began to consider that her ultimate destiny in life was to travel far away, live in a cave in the Himalayas, keep the faith that the gods would come speak to her one day or another, free herself from everything that surrounded her at that moment and that she found boring, so boring.

Without getting into detail, she asked Wilma what she thought of Amsterdam.

"Boring. So boring."

Exactly. Not only Amsterdam but all of Holland, where everyone was born under the protection of the state, no one ever had to worry about becoming a helpless old fogey thanks to all sorts of senior homes and lifetime pensions, health care that was free or practically so, and where recently all the kings had actually been queens—the Queen Mother Wilhelmina; the current queen, Juliana; and the heir to the throne, Beatrix. While women in the United States were burning their bras and demanding equality, Karla—who never used a bra despite the fact her breasts weren't exactly small—was living in a place where such equality had been gained long before, without any noise, without all sorts of attention seeking, by simply following the ancestral logic that power belongs to women—it's they who govern their husbands and children, their presidents and kings, who for their part seek to give the impression that they're exceptional generals, heads of state, businessmen.

Men. They thought they ruled the world but couldn't so much as take a step without, that very same night, seeking the opinions of their partners, lovers, girlfriends, mothers.

Karla needed to take a radical step, discover a country within herself or without that she'd never explored before and find a way past the tedium that she could feel draining her strength with each passing day.

She hoped the tarot reader had been right. If the person she'd been promised didn't show up the next day, she would go to Nepal anyway, alone, running the risk of becoming a "white slave" and ending up sold to some fat sultan in a country where harems were the order of the day—though she had her doubts that anyone would have the courage to do this with her. She would defend herself better than any man, shielding herself from threatening looks, weapon in hand.

She said goodbye to Wilma, they agreed to meet at Paradiso the next day, and she set off for the hostel where she'd spent those monotonous days in Amsterdam, the city of dreams for so many who had crossed the world just to get there. She walked through the narrow streets without sidewalks, her ears alert to hearing something that might be a sort of sign. She wasn't sure what she was waiting for, but signs are always like that, surprising and disguised as routine events. The sensation of the drizzle falling on her face brought her back to reality—not the reality around her but the fact that she was alive, walking down dark alleys in total safety, crossing paths with drug traffickers from Suriname who acted in the shadows—it's true, they posed a real danger to their customers, because they offered the devil's drugs, cocaine and heroin.

She passed through a square—it seemed as if, unlike Rotterdam, the city had a square on every corner. The rain became heavier, and she gave thanks for being able to smile despite all that she had thought about in the coffee shop.

As she walked she uttered silent prayers, words that were neither Lutheran nor Catholic, grateful for the life she had complained about only hours earlier. In her devotion she basked in the sky and earth, the trees and animals, the mere sight of which resolved all the contradictions in her soul and enveloped everything in a deep peace—not the sort of peace that comes from the absence of challenges but the sort that was preparing her for an adventure that she was resolved to see through, regardless of whether she found a travel companion. She was confident that the angels watched over her, singing melodies that, though undetected by her ears, reverberated throughout her and cleansed her mind of impure thoughts, put her in touch with her soul and taught her to love herself though she had never known Love.

I will not feel guilty for what I was thinking before, perhaps it was the film, perhaps the book, but, even if it was only me and my inability to see the beauty that exists inside myself, I ask your forgiveness. I love you and I'm grateful that you always accompany me, that you bless me with your company and free me from the temptations of pleasure and the fear of pain.

Rather unusually, she began to feel guilty for being who she was, living in the country with the highest concentration of museums in the world, crossing at that moment one of the city's 1,281 bridges, gazing at the homes with only three windows on the side (to have more than this was considered ostentatious and an attempt to humiliate the neighbors). She was proud of the laws that governed her people, of their history as seafaring explorers, even if everyone overlooked them for the Spanish and the Portuguese.

They'd made only one bad deal: selling the island of Manhattan to the Americans. But who's perfect?

The night watchman opened the hostel door. She entered as quietly as she could, closed her eyes, and before falling asleep, she thought about the only thing missing in her country.

Mountains.

62

That was it: she would go to the mountains, far from those endless flatlands conquered from the sea by men who knew what they wanted and who had succeeded in taming a landscape that refused to submit.

She decided to wake up earlier than was typical—she was already dressed and ready to go at eleven in the morning, whereas she usually wasn't ready until one in the afternoon. According to the tarot reader, today was the day she would find the person she was looking for, and the clairvoyant could not be wrong; both of them had fallen into a mysterious trance, beyond their control, like most trances, by the way. Layla had said something that hadn't come from her own tongue but from a higher power who'd filled the entire atmosphere of her "office."

There were still very few people in Dam Square—things really began to pick up after noon. But she noticed—finally!—a new face. Hair just like everyone else there, a jacket without many patches (the most prominent was a flag inscribed with BRASIL on top), a bright, knitted shoulder bag, made in South America, which at the time was a hit among the young people who crisscrossed the globe—as were ponchos and beanies that covered the ears. He was smoking a cigarette—a regular one, she knew, since she walked near where he was sitting and couldn't detect any particular smell other than tobacco.

He was terribly busy doing nothing, looking around, at the building at the other end of the square and the hippies scattered about. He must have wanted someone to talk to, but his eyes betrayed shyness—extreme shyness, to be more specific.

She sat at a safe distance, so as to allow her to keep an eye on him and not let him out of her sight before proposing he join her on a trip to Nepal. If he'd already been to Brazil and South America, as his bag suggested, why wouldn't he be interested in going further yet? He must have been about her age, as inexperienced, and it wasn't likely to be difficult to convince him. It didn't matter whether he was ugly or good-looking, fat or thin, tall or short. The only thing that interested her at all was having company on her personal adventure.

aulo, too, had noted the pretty hippie girl who had passed by, and had it not been for his crippling shyness, perhaps he would have dared to flash her a smile. But he lacked the courage—she seemed far away; perhaps she was waiting on someone or wanting only to contemplate the morning free from the sun but not without the threat of rain.

He went back to focusing on the building in front of him, a true architectural marvel, which *Europe on 5 Dollars a Day* described as a royal palace, constructed upon 13,659 piles (also, the guide noted, the entire city was constructed on piles, though no one ever noticed). No guards stood at the door, and tourists went in and out—hordes of them, endless lines, the type of place he would never visit while he was there.

We can always sense when someone is watching us. Paulo could sense that the pretty hippie was now sitting just outside his field of vision, that she hadn't taken her eyes off him. He turned his head, and she was indeed there but began to read as soon as their eyes met.

What to do? For almost a half hour, he sat thinking whether

he ought to get up and go sit at her side—which was what would have been expected in Amsterdam, where people met others without need for excuses and explanations, merely the desire to talk and exchange stories. At the end of this half hour, after repeating a thousand times that he had nothing to lose, that it wouldn't be the first or the last rejection he'd face, he stood up and walked in her direction. Her eyes did not move from her book.

Karla saw him approaching—something unusual in a place where everyone respected others' individual space. He sat down beside her and said the dumbest thing one could say:

"Excuse me."

She sat there looking at him, waiting for him to finish—which he did not. Five awkward minutes later she decided to take the initiative.

"Excuse me *what,* exactly?"

"Nothing."

But, to her joy and relief, he didn't say any of the usual stupid things like "I hope I'm not bothering you," or "What's that building there?" or "You're so beautiful" (foreigners loved to use that one), or "What country are you from?" "Where did you buy these clothes?" that sort of thing.

She decided to help him a bit since she was much more interested in the young man than he could imagine.

"Why the coat of arms with 'Brasil' on your sleeve?"

"In case I come across Brazilians—that's where I come from.

I don't know anyone in the city, and this way they can help me find interesting people."

So this young man, who looked to be intelligent and had dark eyes that shone with an intense energy and a weariness that was even more intense had crossed the Atlantic to meet other Brazilians abroad?

That seemed the very epitome of stupid, but she decided to cut him some slack. She could jump straight to the subject of Nepal and continue the conversation or abandon it once and for all, move to another spot in the square, say she had to meet someone, or even leave without so much as an explanation.

But she decided not to move, and the fact that she stayed sitting there next to Paulo—that was his name—while he considered his options would end up changing her life completely.

That's what love affairs are like—though the last thing she was thinking about at that moment was this secret word and the dangers it brought with it. There they were together, the clairvoyant had been right, the interior and exterior worlds were quickly merging. He could have been feeling the same thing, but he was too shy, it seemed—or perhaps he was only thinking about finding someone to smoke hashish with or, what was worse, saw her as a companion to take to Vondelpark to make love and then go their separate ways as if nothing very important had happened beyond an orgasm.

How to determine what someone is or isn't in a matter of minutes? Of course, we know when a person repulses us, and we quickly distance ourselves, but this certainly wasn't the case. He was crazy skinny, and he seemed to wash his hair. He must have showered that morning, she could still smell the soap on his body.

The second he sat down beside her and uttered that stupid phrase "Excuse me," Karla had felt a deep sense of well-being, as though she were no longer alone. She was with him, and he with her, and they both knew this—even though nothing more had been said and neither of them was sure what was happening. Their unconfessed sentiments had yet to be revealed, but they would not remain unknown for long, Paulo and Karla were merely waiting for the right moment to make their feelings clear. That was the instant when many relationships that could have resulted in great love stories were lost—or because when two souls meet on the face of the earth, they already know where their journeys will lead them and this terrifies them, or because we are so focused on our own things that we don't even allow two souls the time to get to know each other. We set off in search of "something better" and lose the opportunity of a lifetime.

Karla was allowing her soul to bare itself. At times, we are fooled by their words because our souls aren't exactly very faithful and end up accepting situations that in reality don't have anything to do with anything; they try to please the mind and ignore the thing into which Karla was plunging deeper and deeper: Understanding. The outer self, that which you believe yourself to be, is nothing more than a limiting place, a stranger to the true self. This is why people have such a hard time listening to what their souls are telling them; they try to control the soul so that it does exactly as they have already decided—their wants, their hopes, their futures, the desire to say to friends, "I finally found the love of my life," the dread of ending up alone in an old folks' home.

She could no longer pretend. She didn't know what she was feeling and sought to leave things as they were, without any detailed justifications or explanations. She was aware that she ought to finally lift the veil concealing her heart, but she didn't know how and wasn't about to find out so soon. It would be ideal to keep him at a safe distance until she could see what happened between the two in the coming hours, days, or years—no, she wasn't thinking of years, because her destination was a cave in Kathmandu, alone, in touch with the universe.

aulo's soul had not yet bared itself, and he had no way of knowing if the girl before him would disappear from one moment to the next. He didn't know what else to say, she too got quiet, and they both had accepted that silence and kept their gazes straight ahead, without actually noting anything. Around them, people were on their way to lunch counters and restaurants, packed trolleys rolled on by, but both Paulo and Karla looked lost, their emotions in some other dimension.

"Would you like to get lunch?"

Taking that as an invitation, Paulo was pleasantly surprised. He couldn't understand why such a beautiful girl was asking him to lunch—his first few hours in Amsterdam were off to a good start.

He hadn't planned anything like that, and when things happen without planning or expectations they are that much more enjoyable and worthwhile—talking to a stranger without an eye to any romantic connection had allowed things to flow more naturally.

Was she alone? How long would she continue to pay attention to him? What did he need to do to keep her by his side?

Nothing. The sequence of stupid questions disappeared into thin air, and even though he had just had something to eat, he was going to have lunch with her. His only worry was that she might pick an expensive restaurant, and he needed to make his money last a year, until the date on his return ticket.

Pilgrim, your thoughts wander; set your mind at rest.
Not all those summoned are to be the chosen ones
It is not just anyone who sleeps with a smile on his lips
Who sees what you see now.

Of course we need to share. Even if it's something everyone already knows, it's important that we don't allow ourselves to be swept away by selfish thoughts of being the sole person to arrive at the end of the journey. Whoever does this finds an empty paradise, without anything particularly interesting, and soon finds himself dying of boredom.

We cannot take the lamps that light the way and carry them with us.

If we do this, we end up filling our backpacks with lanterns. In that case, even with all the light we carry, we still won't have any company to speak of. What good is that?

But it was difficult to keep his mind at rest—he needed to write down everything that was happening around him. A revolution without arms, a road without border checkpoints or dangerous turns. A world that had suddenly become young, independent of people's ages or their religious and political beliefs. The sun had come out, as though to say that finally the Renaissance was making a return, to change everyone's habits and customs—and one day very soon, people would no longer depend on the opinions of others but rather on their own ways of seeing life.

People dressed in yellow, dancing and singing in the street, clothing of all colors, a girl handing out roses to passersby, everyone smiling—yes, tomorrow would be a better day, despite what was happening in Latin America and other countries. Tomorrow would be better simply because there was no other choice, there was no way to return to the past and again allow puritanism, hypocrisy, and lies to fill the days and nights of those who walked on this earth. He thought back to his exorcism on the train and the thousands of reproaches everyone directed his way, those he knew and those he didn't. He thought back to the way his parents suffered and felt like calling home right away to say:

Don't worry, I'm happy, and soon you will understand why I wasn't born to go to college, earn a diploma, and get a job. I was born to be free and I can survive this way. I will always have something to do, I will always find a way to make money, I can always get married one day and start a family, but now is not the time for that—it's time for me to try to live only in the present, here and now, with the joy of children, to whom Jesus bequeathed the Kingdom of Heaven. If I need to find a job as a laborer, I'll do this without complaining because it will allow me to live in communion with the earth, the sun, and rain. If one day I need to lock myself in an office, I will also do this without complaining, because I'll have others at my side, we'll form a group, a group that will discover how good it is to sit around a table and talk, pray, laugh, and wash ourselves clean of all those afternoons of repetitive work. If I need to be alone, I'll do that, too; if I fall in love and decide to marry I'll get married, for I'm certain that my wife, the woman who is to be the love of my life, will accept my joy as the greatest blessing a man can give to a woman.

The young woman at his side stopped, bought some flowers, and instead of taking them somewhere, formed them into two circles, placing one on his head and the other on hers. Far from seeming ridiculous, it was a way of celebrating the small victories in life, in the same way the Greeks, millennia earlier, had exalted their victors and heroes—with crowns not of gold but of laurels. They may have wilted away but they weren't heavy and didn't demand the constant vigilance of the crowns of kings and queens. Many people passing them by donned this sort of crown, making everything more beautiful.

People played on wooden flutes, violins, guitars, sitars—it made for a jumbled soundtrack but one that felt natural to that street without sidewalks, a street like most of the city's thoroughfares: full of bicycles, time slowing down and then speeding back up. Paulo was afraid that this speeding up would soon win out and the dream would come to an end.

He was walking not through the street, but through a dream in which the people were flesh and bone. They spoke unfamiliar languages, turned to see the woman at his side, and smiled on account of her beauty; she would return the gesture, and he would feel a spike of jealousy that was soon replaced by pride at the fact she had picked him for a companion.

Every now and then someone offered him incense, bracelets, colorful coats, possibly from Peru or Bolivia, and he felt like buying it all because they returned his smiles and neither took offense nor insisted too much the way salespeople at stores did. If he bought something, perhaps this would mean one more night for them, one more day in paradise—though he knew that everyone, absolutely everyone, found a way to survive in this world. Paulo needed to save as much as possible and also try to discover a way to live in that city until his plane ticket began to weigh down the little elastic belt hidden around his waist, telling him that it was time, that he needed to snap out of the dream and come back to reality.

A reality that even appeared from time to time on those streets and parks, on little tables with posters behind them showing the atrocities committed in Vietnam—a photo of a general executing a Vietcong in cold blood. All they asked was that passersby sign a petition, and everyone cooperated.

At that moment he realized that the Renaissance was still a long way from taking over the world, but it had begun, yes, it had begun. Not a one of those young people—of the many young people on the street—would forget what they were experiencing, and when they returned to their countries they would become evangelists for peace and love. It was all possible, a world finally free of oppression, hate, husbands who beat their wives, torturers who hung people upside down and killed them slowly with . . .

. . . Not that he'd lost his sense of justice—he was still taken aback with the injustice throughout the world—but he needed to rest and regain his strength, at least for the time being. He had spent a good part of his youth afraid of everything, now was the time to show courage in the face of life and the unfamiliar path he was about to tread.

They walked into one of dozens of stores selling pipes, multi-colored shawls, statues of Eastern saints, patches. Paulo bought what he was looking for: a series of star-shaped metal appliqués he would fasten to his jacket when he got back to the hostel.

In one of the city's many parks, there were three girls without shirts or bras, their eyes closed, holding a yoga pose, facing the sun, which threatened to dip behind clouds before long, and it would be two full seasons yet until spring returned. He looked closer and saw the town square full of older people, coming and going from work, people who didn't so much as bother to look at the girls—because nudity was neither illegal nor frowned upon, each person's body was his or her own business and it was up to each of them to decide what was best.

And the T-shirts, the T-shirts were walking billboards, some with images of icons like Jimi Hendrix, Jim Morrison, Janis Joplin. But the majority announced the Renaissance:

> Today is the first day of the rest of your life.
> A single dream is more powerful than a thousand realities.
> Every great dream begins with a dreamer.

One in particular caught his eye:

> *A dream is something unpredictable and dangerous for those*
> *who lack the courage to dream.*

Right. This was what the system did not tolerate, but the dream would win out in the end, and before the Americans were defeated in Vietnam.

He believed. He had chosen his madness and now intended to live it fully, staying there until he heard his calling to do something that helped to change the world. His dream was to be a writer, but it was still early, and he had his doubts whether books had this power, but he would do his best to show others what they could not see.

One thing was certain: there was no turning back. Now, there was only the path of light.

He met a Brazilian couple, Tiago and Tabita, who had noticed the flag on his coat and introduced themselves.

"We're Children of God," they said and invited him to visit the place where they lived.

We're all Children of God, aren't we?

Yes, but they were part of a cult whose founder had experienced a revelation. Would he like to know more?

Paulo assured them he would; when Karla decided to leave him before the day was out, he'd already have new friends.

———

But, as soon as they parted, Karla grabbed the patch on his jacket and tore it straight off.

"You already bought what you were looking for—stars are much more beautiful than flags. If you want, I can help you put them on in the shape of an Egyptian cross or the peace sign."

"You didn't need to do that. All you had to do was ask and let me decide if I wanted to go on wearing the patch on my sleeve or not. I love and hate my country, but that's my problem. I just met you, and if you think that you can tell me what to do—to give me orders—because you think I'm somehow dependent on the only person I've actually met here, better we go our separate ways now. It can't be all that hard to find an affordable restaurant around here."

His tone had hardened, and caught off guard, Karla considered his reaction a good thing. He wasn't some dimwit who simply did what others told him, even when he was in a city he did not know. He must have been through quite a bit in his life.

She handed him the patch.

"Put it somewhere else. It's rude to speak in a language I don't understand, and it takes a lack of imagination to come so far only to meet up with people you can find back home. If you start in with the Portuguese again, I'll switch to Dutch, and that, I think, will be the end of our conversation."

The restaurant wasn't simply cheap—it was *free,* this magic word that tends to make everything taste much better.

"Who pays for all this? The Dutch government?"

"The Dutch government doesn't let a single one of its citizens go hungry, but in this case the money comes from George Harrison, who's adopted our religion."

Karla listened with a mix of feigned interest and clear boredom. The silence they'd maintained as they walked had confirmed what the clairvoyant had told her the day before: the young man was the perfect companion for a trip to Nepal—he didn't speak much, never sought to force his opinions on others, but he knew exactly how to fight for what was his, as she'd seen with the flag patch. She needed only to find the right moment to broach the subject.

They walked over to the buffet and filled their plates with several tasty vegetarian dishes while they listened to one of the people dressed in orange explain who they were to those who had just arrived. There must have been many of them, and converting someone at that time was ridiculously simple since Westerners worshiped everything that came from the exotic East.

"You must have met some of the people from our group on your way here," said a man who looked a bit older, with a white beard and the saintly air of someone who had never sinned in his entire life. "The original name of our religion is quite difficult, so you can just call us Hare Krishna—that's how we've been known for centuries, since we believe that repeating 'Hare Krishna, Hare Rama' empties our minds, leaving room for energy to enter. We believe that everything is one, we share a single soul, and each drop of light in this soul spreads to the dark spots that surround it. That's it. Whoever wants to can grab a Bhagavad Gita on their way out and fill out a form requesting to join our group. You shall lack nothing—that was our Enlightened Lord's promise before the great battle, when one of the warriors was racked with guilt for taking part in a civil war. The Enlightened Lord responded that no one kills and no one dies—his only responsibility is to fulfill his duty and do as he has been told."

The man grabbed one of the books in question: Paulo stared intently at the guru, and Karla stared intently at Paulo—though she doubted he hadn't heard all this before.

"O son of Kuntī, either you will be killed on the battlefield and attain the heavenly planets, or you will conquer and enjoy the earthly kingdom. Therefore, get up with determination and fight."

The guru closed the book.

"This is what we have to do. Instead of wasting our time saying 'This is good' or 'This is bad,' we need to fulfill our destiny. It was destiny that brought the two of you here today. Whoever wishes can come with us to dance and sing in the streets soon after we've finished eating."

Paulo's eyes lit up, and there was no need for him to say a thing. Karla had understood everything.

"You're not thinking about joining them, are you?"

"Of course I am. I never sang and danced in the streets like that."

"Did you know they only allow sex after marriage, and even then only for the purpose of procreation and not pleasure? Can you believe that a group that claims such enlightenment would be capable of rejecting, denying, or condemning something so beautiful?"

"I'm not thinking about sex, I'm thinking about dancing and singing. It's been forever since I last heard music or sang, and this is a black hole in my life."

"I can take you out singing and dancing tonight."

Why did that girl seem so interested in him? She could get any man she wanted whenever she wanted. He thought back to his Argentinean friend—perhaps she needed someone to help her with a job that he wasn't the least bit interested in. He decided to test the waters.

"Do you know the House of Rising Sun?"

His question could be interpreted three ways: first, whether she was familiar with the song ("The House of the Rising Sun," the Animals). Second, if she knew what the song meant. Third, and finally, if she would like to go there.

"Quit messing around."

This boy, whom at first she'd judged to be so intelligent, so charming, quiet, easy to control, seemed to have misunderstood everything. And, incredible though it may seem, she needed him more than he needed her.

"All right then. Go with them and I'll follow close behind. We'll find each other at the end."

She felt like adding, "I already had my Hare Krishna phase," but she restrained herself so as not to scare her prey.

It was so much fun to be there jumping around, leaping to and fro, singing at the top of his lungs, following those people who dressed in orange, rang little bells, and seemed to be at peace with their lives. Five others had decided to join the group, too, and as they made their way through the streets, still more joined in. He didn't want to lose her; the two of them had come together for some mysterious reason, a mystery that needed to be kept intact—never understood, but maintained. Yes, there she was, a safe distance behind, so as to avoid being seen with the monks or the apprentice monks, and each time their eyes met, they smiled at one another.

The tie between them was being forged and strengthened.

He remembered a story from his childhood, "The Pied Piper of Hamelin," in which the main character, to get revenge on a city that had promised to pay him and then did not, decided to hypnotize the town's children and lead them far away with the power of his music. That's what was happening at that moment—Paulo had become a child and was dancing in the middle of the street, everything so different from the years he'd spent deep in books about magic, performing complicated rituals and believing that he was closing in on the true avatars. Perhaps he was, perhaps he wasn't, but dancing and singing also helped to reach the same state of mind.

After so much jumping up and down and repeating the mantra, he began to enter a state in which thought, logic, and the city streets no longer held so much importance—his mind was entirely clear, and he came back to reality only from time to time, to make sure Karla was close behind. Yes, he could see her, and it would be a very good thing if she remained in his life for a long time to come, even if he had known her for only three hours.

He was certain that the same thing had happened to her—or else she would have simply left him at the restaurant.

He was beginning to understand the words Krishna had said to the warrior Arjuna before battle. It wasn't exactly what was written in the book but in her soul:

Fight because you need to fight, because you're facing a battle.

Fight because you are at peace with the universe, with the planets, the suns that explode and the stars that shrink and flare out forever.

Fight to fulfill your destiny, without giving thought to gain or profit, losses or stratagems, victories or defeats.

Seek not your own gratification, but that of the Supreme Love who offers nothing beyond a glimmering contact with the Cosmos and thus demands an act of complete devotion—without doubts, without questions, love for love's sake and nothing else.

A love that owes nothing to anyone, that has no obligations, that finds joy in simple existence and the freedom to express itself.

The procession arrived in Dam Square and began to circle the plaza. Paulo decided to stop there, allow the girl he had met to return to his side—she seemed different, more relaxed, more at ease in his presence. The sun wasn't quite so hot as before, it was unlikely he'd see the girls with their bare breasts again, but since everything seemed to contradict his expectations, the couple noted bright lights to the left of the spot where they were seated. Having absolutely nothing to do, they decided to go see what was happening.

The reflectors cast light across the body of a completely nude model holding a tulip that covered only her crotch. The obelisk in the center of Dam Square formed the background behind her. Karla asked one of the assistants what the meaning of all that was.

"A poster for the department of tourism."

"This is how you're selling Holland to foreigners? A place where people go naked in the city?"

The assistant turned and walked away without answering her question. At that moment, the crew took a break and Karla turned to another assistant while the makeup artist stepped in to retouch the model's right breast. She repeated her question. The man, a bit stressed, asked her not to interrupt his work, but Karla knew what he wanted.

"You seem tense. What's worrying you?"

"The light. The light's almost gone; before long the square will be dark," the assistant responded, trying to rid himself of this impertinent girl.

"You're not from here, are you? It's early fall, it stays light out until seven. Not to mention, I have the power to stop the sun."

The man gave her a look of surprise. She'd gotten what she wanted: his attention.

"Why are you making a poster with a naked woman holding a tulip over her crotch? Is this the image of Holland you want to show the rest of the world?"

He responded with a tone of thinly veiled irritation:

"What Holland? Who said you're in Holland, a country where the houses have low-set windows that open onto the street and lace curtains that allow anyone to see what's going on inside, because after all, there are no sinners here, each family is an open book? That's Holland, my dear: a country overrun by Calvinists, where everyone is a sinner until proven the contrary, sin resides in the heart, mind, body, emotions. A country where only the grace of God can save anyone, but not everyone, just the chosen. You're from here—haven't you understood this yet?"

He lit a cigarette and watched the girl who, so arrogant before, now wore a look that betrayed intimidation.

"This isn't Holland, my child, this is Amsterdam, with prostitutes in the windows and drugs on the streets—surrounded by an invisible cordon sanitaire. Woe to they who seek to take these ideas beyond the city. Not only are they unwelcome, they won't even manage a hotel room if they're not dressed properly. But you know this, don't you? So please step aside and let us work."

It was the man who stepped aside, leaving Karla looking as if she had just taken a sucker punch. Paulo tried to console her, but she just muttered to herself.

"It's true. He's right, it's all true."

How could it be true? The border guards wore earrings!

"There's an invisible wall around the city," she told him. "You want to get crazy? Well then, we'll find a place where everyone can do almost everything they want, but don't overstep these bounds or you'll be arrested for drug trafficking, even if you're merely consuming, or for public indecency, because you ought to be wearing a bra, keeping your modesty and morality intact, or else this country will never move forward."

Paulo was a bit taken aback. He began to distance himself.

"Meet me back here at nine tonight—I promised I was going to take you to hear some real music and go dancing."

"There's no need . . ."

"Of course there is. Don't stand me up, no man ever bailed on me and ran."

Karla had her doubts—she regretted not having taken part in the dancing and singing through the streets, it would have brought them closer. But whatever, these are the risks any couple must run.

Couple?

"I've spent my life believing whatever people tell me and I always end up disappointed," she often heard others say. "Does that ever happen to you?"

Of course it happened, but now, at twenty-three, she was better at watching out for herself. The only other option—besides trusting in others—was to transform herself into someone who was always on the defensive, incapable of loving, making decisions, always transferring the blame for everything that went wrong onto others. What was the point in living like that?

Those who trust in themselves trust others. Because they

know that, when they are betrayed—and everyone is betrayed, that's part of life—it's possible to start all over again. Part of the fun in life is exactly this: running risks.

The nightclub Karla had invited Paulo to, which went by the suggestive name of Paradiso, was in fact a . . . church. A nineteenth-century church, originally built to house a local religious group that, already in the fifties, realized it had lost its power to attract new followers, despite being a sort of reform of Luther's reform. In 1965, in light of the costs of maintaining the church, the few remaining faithful decided to abandon the building, occupied two years later by hippies who found in its nave the perfect spot for discussions, workshops, concerts, and political activities.

The police evicted them a short time later, but the place remained empty and the hippies returned en masse—the only solution was either to resort to violence or to allow things to go on as they had. An agreement between the long-haired libertines and the impeccably dressed city officials allowed the hippies to build a stage where the altar once stood, as long as they paid taxes on each ticket sold and were careful not to destroy the stained-glass windows along the back wall.

The taxes, of course, were never paid—the organizers always alleged that the space's cultural activities operated at a loss, and no one seemed to care or even think about another eviction. On the other hand, the stained-glass windows were kept clean, the tiniest of cracks soon repaired with lead and stained glass, and so continued to show the glory and beauty of the King of

Kings. When asked why they showed such care, those responsible answered:

"Because they're beautiful. And it required a lot of work to design them, make them, put them into place—we're here to put our art on display, and we respect the art of those who came before us."

When they walked in, people were dancing to the sound of one of the hits of that era. The towering ceiling didn't make for the best of acoustics, but what did it matter? Had Paulo given a thought to acoustics when he was singing "Hare Krishna" in the streets? What mattered was seeing everyone smiling, laughing, smoking, trading looks that spelled seduction or perhaps mere admiration. At that point, no one needed to pay an entry fee or taxes—the city government had taken it upon itself to not only avoid any lawlessness but care for the property, now subsidized.

By the looks of it, apart from the naked woman with the tulip covering her crotch, there was great interest in transforming Amsterdam into some sort of cultural capital—the hippies had revived the city, and the hotels, according to Karla, were now filling up; everyone wanted to catch a glimpse of the leaderless tribe whose women, it was said (falsely, of course), were always ready to make love with the first man who appeared before them.

"The Dutch are smart."

"Of course we are. We've already conquered the entire world, including Brazil."

They climbed up to one of the balconies that circled the nave.

A miraculous acoustic dead spot meant they could talk a bit there without the interference of the blaring noise below. But neither Paulo nor Karla felt like talking—they leaned over the wooden safety rail and sat watching the people dance. She suggested they go down and do the same, but Paulo said that the only music he really knew how to dance to was *"Hare Krishna, Hare Rama."* They both laughed, lit a cigarette, which they shared, and then Karla waved someone over—through the cloud of smoke, he could see it was another girl.

"Wilma," she introduced herself.

"We're headed to Nepal," Karla said. Paulo laughed.

Wilma was startled by Karla's comment but did nothing to give that away. Karla excused herself to go talk with her friend in Dutch, and Paulo sat watching the people dance below.

Nepal? So the girl he'd just met and who seemed to like his company was about to leave? And she'd said "we," as though she already had company for such an adventure. And to such a far-off place, with a ticket that must have cost a fortune?

He was loving Amsterdam, but he knew why: he wasn't alone. There was no need to make conversation with anyone, as soon as he'd arrived he'd found some company, and he would have liked to explore all that there was to see there with her at his side. To say that he was falling in love would be an exaggeration, but Karla had the kind of attitude he liked—she knew exactly where she wanted to go.

But Nepal? With another girl, whom even if he didn't want to he would end up watching over and protecting—because that was how his parents had raised him? It was beyond his financial means. He knew that sooner or later he would have to leave this magical place, and his next stop—if the local customs officials allowed it—would be Piccadilly Circus and all the people from around the world who were to be found there.

Karla was still talking to her friend, and he pretended to be interested in the music below: Simon & Garfunkel, the Beatles, James Taylor, Santana, Carly Simon, Joe Cocker, B. B. King, Creedence Clearwater Revival—a long list that continued to grow with each month, each day, each hour. There was always the Brazilian couple he'd met earlier that afternoon, and they might introduce him to other people—but let someone leave just as soon as she'd entered his life?

He listened to the familiar chords of the Animals and remembered that he'd asked Karla to take him to a house of the rising sun. The end of the song was terrifying, he knew what the lyrics meant, but even so the danger fascinated and beckoned to him.

Spend your lives in sin and misery
In the House of the Rising Sun

The idea had come to her all of a sudden, Karla explained to Wilma.

"It's a good thing you controlled yourself. You could have ruined everything."

"Nepal?"

"That's right. One day I'm going to be old, fat, living with a jealous husband and children who make it impossible for me to take care of myself, working an office job that's the same thing day in, day out, and I'll get used to that: the routine, the comfort, the place I'm living. I can always go back to Rotterdam. I can always take advantage of the wonders of unemployment insurance or social security that our country provides. I can always become CEO of Shell, or Philips, or Heineken, because I'm Dutch and they only trust people from their own country. But Nepal is now or never—I'm already getting old."

"At twenty-three?"

"The years pass faster than you think, Wilma, and I'd advise you to do the same. Take risks now, when you still have your health and some courage. We both agree Amsterdam is boring as can be, but we think this because we've gotten used to it. Today, when I saw this Brazilian guy, the way his eyes lit up, I discovered I was the boring one. I could no longer see the beauty of freedom because I'd become used to it."

She looked to the side and saw Paulo with his eyes closed, listening to "Stand by Me." Then she continued.

"So I need to recover some beauty—just that. To know that, though I'll come back one day, there are still many things I haven't seen or experienced. Where will my heart lead if I've yet to wander so many unknown paths? Where will I end up next, if I have yet to leave here like I should? What hills will I climb if I'm blind to the rope before me? I came from Rotterdam to Amsterdam with this purpose, I tried convincing several men to continue on toward the paths that don't exist, ships that never reach any port, a sky without limits, but they all refused—they all were afraid either of me or of our unknown destination. Until this afternoon, when I met the Brazilian guy; regardless of what I thought about it, he followed the Hare Krishna through the streets, singing and dancing. I felt like doing the same thing, but my worries about looking like a strong woman stopped me. But I'm done doubting."

Wilma still didn't understand exactly why Nepal, or how Paulo had helped Karla.

"When you showed up and I mentioned Nepal, I sensed it was the right thing to do. At that same moment, I noticed he wasn't only surprised, but afraid. The goddess must have inspired me to say this. I'm not anxious the way I was this morning, the way I've been the whole week—when I even came to doubt that I'd be able to fulfill this dream."

"You've had this dream for a long time?"

"No. It began as an ad clipped from one of the alternative newspapers. Ever since, it's all I can think about."

Wilma was going to ask her if she'd smoked too much hashish that day, but just then Paulo showed up.

"Let's dance?" he asked.

She took his hand and they walked down together to the church's nave. Wilma wasn't sure where to go, but that wouldn't be a problem for long; as soon as someone noticed she was alone, they would come and start a conversation—everyone spoke to everyone there.

When they walked out into the silent drizzle, their ears were still buzzing from the music. They yelled so they could hear one another.

"Are you going to be around tomorrow?"

"I'll be in the same spot you found me the first time. Then I need to go buy the bus ticket to Nepal."

Again with this Nepal stuff? A bus ticket?

"You can come along, if you'd like," she said as though she were doing him a huge favor. "But I'd like to take you on a little outing just outside Amsterdam. Have you ever seen a windmill?"

She laughed at her own question—that was how the rest of the world thought of her country: clogs, windmills, cows, prostitutes in the windows.

"We can meet in the same spot we always do," Paulo responded, a bit anxious and a bit pleased with himself because she—that model of beauty, her hair neatly combed and full of flowers, a long skirt, a vest covered in mirrors, patchouli perfume, a wonder from head to toe—wanted to see him again.

"I'll be there around one o'clock. I have to get a bit of sleep. But weren't we going to one of those houses of the rising sun?"

"I told you I'd show you where to find one. I didn't say I'd go with you."

They walked about five hundred feet until they reached an alley where there was a door without any number or music coming from it.

"There's one over there. I'd like to give you two suggestions." She had thought about using the word "advice," but that would have been the worst choice in the world.

"Don't leave there with anything—there must be some policemen we can't see in one of these windows, keeping an eye on everyone who visits the location. And they tend to search anyone who leaves. And whoever leaves with anything goes straight to the slammer."

Paulo nodded, he understood, and asked what her second suggestion was.

"Don't try anything either."

Having said this, she kissed him on the lips—an innocent kiss that promised much but surrendered little. Then she turned around and set off toward her hostel. Paulo stood there alone, asking himself whether he ought to enter. Perhaps it was better to go back to his hostel and start gluing the metallic stars he'd bought that afternoon to his jacket.

However, his curiosity won out, and he walked toward the door.

The hallway was narrow, poorly lit, the ceiling low. At the end of it, a man with a shaved head who clearly had experience as a policeman in some country sized him up—the famous "body language test," used to gauge a person's intentions, degree of anxiety, financial standing, and profession. He asked Paulo if he had money to spend. Yes, but he wasn't about to do as he had done at customs and try to show him how much. The man hesitated for a moment then let him pass—he couldn't have been a tourist, tourists weren't interested in that sort of thing.

There were people lying on mattresses spread across the floor, others leaning against the red painted walls. What was he doing there? Satisfying some morbid curiosity?

No one was talking or listening to music. Even his morbid curiosity was limited to what he could see, and that was the same glimmer—or lack of glimmer—in everyone's eyes. He tried to talk to one kid his age, his skin emaciated and spots on his face and shirtless body, as though he'd been bitten by some insect and scratched himself until the bites became red and swollen.

Another man came in—he looked ten years older than most of the kids outside, but he must still have been approaching Paulo's age. He was—at least for the moment—the only one sober. A short time later he would be in another universe, and Paulo walked up to him to see if he could come away with something, even if it were a simple phrase for the book he intended to write in the future—his dream was to become a writer, and he had paid a high price for this: stints in psychiatric hospitals, prison and torture, the prohibition from the mother of his teenage girlfriend that she get anywhere near him, the scorn of his classmates when they saw he had begun to dress differently.

And—his revenge—the jealousy they all felt when he got his first girlfriend—beautiful and rich—and began to travel the world.

But why was he thinking only about himself in such a decrepit environment? Because he needed to talk to someone there. He sat next to the oldish young man. He watched him pull out a spoon with its handle bent and a syringe that looked like it had been used many times.

"I wanted to . . ."

The oldish young man got up to go sit in another corner, but Paulo took the equivalent of three or four dollars from his pocket and set them on the floor next to the spoon. He was met with a look of surprise.

"Are you police?"

"No, I'm not police, I'm not even Dutch. I would just like to . . ."

"You a journalist?"

"No. I'm a writer. That's why I'm here."

"What books did you write?"

"None yet. First I need to do some research."

The other man looked at the money on the floor and then again at Paulo, doubting that a person so young could be writing something—unless it was for the newspapers that were part of the "Invisible Post." He reached for the money, but Paulo stopped him.

"Just five minutes. Not more than five minutes."

The oldish young man agreed—no one had ever paid a cent for his time ever since he threw away a promising career as an executive at a multinational bank, ever since he tried the "kiss of the needle" for the first time.

The kiss of the needle?

"That's right. We prick ourselves a few times before injecting the heroin because what everyone else calls pain is our prelude to finding something all of you will never understand."

They were whispering so as not to draw the attention of others, but Paulo knew that even if an atomic bomb dropped on the place none of the people there would go to the trouble of fleeing.

"You can't use my name."

The other man had begun to open up, and five minutes passed quickly. Paulo could sense the devil's presence in that house.

"And then what? What's it feel like?"

"And then I can't describe it—you only know by trying it. Or believing what Lou Reed and the Velvet Underground said about it."

Cause it makes me feel like I'm a man
When I put a spike into my vein

Paulo had listened to Lou Reed before. That wasn't gonna cut it.

"Please, try to describe it. Our five minutes are going fast."

The man before him took a deep breath. He kept one eye on Paulo and the other on his syringe. He should respond quickly and get rid of the impertinent "writer" before he got kicked out of the house, taking the money with him.

"I'm guessing you have some experience with drugs. I'm familiar with the effects of hashish and marijuana: peace and euphoria, self-confidence, an urge to eat and make love. I don't care about any of these, they're things from a kind of life we've been taught to live. You smoke hash and think: 'The world is a beautiful place, I'm finally paying attention,' but depending on the dose, you end up on a trip that takes you straight to hell. You take LSD and think: Good god, how didn't I notice that before, the earth breathes and its colors are constantly changing? Is that what you want to know?"

That's what he wanted to know. But he waited for the oldish young man to continue his story.

"With heroin, it's completely different: you're in control of everything—your body, your mind, your art. An immense, indescribable happiness washes over the entire universe. Christ on earth. Krishna in your veins. Buddha smiling down on you from heaven. No hallucinations, this is reality, true reality. Do you believe me?"

Paulo didn't. But he didn't say anything, merely nodded.

"The next day, there's no hangover, just the feeling that you've been to paradise and come back to this crappy world. Then you go to work and it hits you that everything is a lie, people trying to justify their lives, look important, creating obstacles because it gives them a sense of authority, of power. You can't stand all the hypocrisy anymore and decide to go back to paradise, but paradise is expensive, the gate is narrow. Whoever visits discovers that life is beautiful, that the sun can in fact be divided into rays, it's no longer that boring, round ball you can't even look at. The next day, you go back to work on a train full of people with empty looks, emptier than the looks of the people here. Everybody thinking about getting home, making dinner, turning on the television, escaping reality—man, reality is this white powder, not the television!"

The longer the oldish young man spoke, the more Paulo felt like trying it at least one time, just this once. The figure before him knew this.

"With hashish, I know there's a world there that I don't belong to. The same with LSD. But heroin, man, heroin's my thing. It's what makes life worth living, no matter what the people outside say. There's just one problem . . ."

Finally—a problem. Paulo needed to hear about this problem right away, because he was a few inches from the tip of a needle and his first experience with heroin.

"The problem is your body builds up a tolerance. At first, I was spending five dollars a day; today it takes twenty dollars to get to paradise. I already sold everything I had—my next step is to beg on the streets; after begging I'll have to steal, because the devil doesn't like people who've been to paradise. I know what's going to happen, because it's happened to everyone you see here today. But I don't care."

How strange. Everyone had a different idea about which side the gate to paradise was to be found on.

"I think the five minutes are up."

"Yep, you explained things pretty well, and I'm grateful."

"When you write about this, don't be like the others, who live their lives judging what they don't understand. Be true. Use your imagination to fill in the gaps."

The conversation had come to a close, but Paulo stayed where he was. The oldish young man didn't seem to mind—he stuffed the money in his pocket and thought that if Paulo had paid, he had the right to watch.

He put some white powder on the bent spoon and positioned his lighter beneath it. Little by little, the powder began to turn to liquid and boil. The man asked Paulo to help him put the strap around his arm until his vein protruded beneath the skin.

"Some don't have anywhere else to put it, they inject themselves in the foot, in the back of the hand, but—thank God— I still have a long road ahead of me."

He filled the syringe with the liquid from the spoon and, exactly like he'd said at the beginning of his story, stuck the needle in several times, anticipating the moment when he would open the so-called gate. Finally, he injected the liquid, and his eyes lost their anxious look, they turned angelic, and then five or ten minutes later they lost their glimmer and honed in on some spot off in space where, if he was to be believed, Buddha, Krishna, and Jesus must have been floating around.

Paulo got up, and skipping over bodies sprawled across dirty mattresses, making as little noise as possible, he headed for the exit, but the security guard with the shaved head blocked his exit.

"You just got here. Leaving so soon?"

"Yeah, I don't have the money for this."

"Liar. Someone saw you giving a few bucks to Ted [that must have been the name of the oldish young man he'd spoken with]. You come here searching for clients?"

"Not at all. I just spoke with one person, later you can ask him what we talked about."

Paulo made to leave again, but the giant's body blocked his way. He was starting to worry, though he knew that nothing bad could happen; Karla had told him that outside, through the windows, the police kept an eye on the place.

"A friend of mine would like to talk to you," the giant said, pointing to a door in the back of the large room, making it clear with his tone of voice that it was best that Paulo obey. Perhaps Karla had made up the story about the police to keep him from worrying.

Seeing he didn't have much choice, he walked toward the door. Before he had arrived, the door opened, revealing a man with Elvis Presley–style hair and sideburns, in understated dress. In a friendly voice, the man asked Paulo to come in and offered him a chair.

The office looked nothing like what Paulo was used to seeing in the movies: scantily clad women, champagne, men with dark sunglasses carrying high-caliber weapons. On the contrary, the office was nondescript—painted white, with some cheap reproductions on the wall and nothing atop the desk except for a telephone. Right behind the desk—an old but carefully preserved piece of furniture—was a huge photo.

"The Belém Tower," Paulo said in Portuguese, without realizing he'd just spoken in his native language.

"Exatamente," the man responded, also in Portuguese. "From that point, we set off to conquer the world. Can I offer you a drink?"

No thanks. His heart still hadn't returned to normal.

"Okay, well, I imagine you're a busy person," the man continued, using an expression which was entirely out of context but which suggested a certain kindness. "We noticed that you came in, left, spoke only with a single one of our clients, and you don't look like an undercover cop, but a person who, after quite the effort, has managed to make it to this city and enjoy everything it has to offer."

Paulo said nothing.

"Nor did you show any interest in the excellent product we offer here. Would you mind showing me your passport?"

Of course he minded, but he wasn't about to refuse. He stuck his hand into the elastic belt around his waist, removed the passport, and held it out in front of the man. He immediately regretted this—what if the man took it?

But the mysterious figure merely flipped through its pages, smiled, and gave it back.

"Ah, only a few countries—terrific. Peru, Bolivia, Chile, Argentina, Italy. Not to mention Holland, of course. I imagine you must have passed border security without any trouble."

None at all.

"Where are you headed now?"

"England."

It was the only thing that had occurred to him, though he had no intention of giving that man his complete itinerary.

"I'd like to make you an offer. I need to move some product—

I imagine you might guess what it is—to Düsseldorf, Germany. It's only five pounds, which you could easily fit underneath your shirt. We'd buy you a larger sweater, of course; everyone uses a sweater and jacket in the winter. By the way, pretty soon this jacket of yours isn't going to do you much good against the weather—fall is coming."

Paulo simply waited to hear the man's proposal.

"We'll pay you five thousand dollars—half in Amsterdam and the other half when you deliver the product to our supplier in Germany. You only need to cross one border, nothing more. Without a doubt, this will make for a much more comfortable trip to England. Border officials there tend to be rather strict; they generally ask to see how much money a 'tourist' is carrying."

Paulo couldn't possibly have heard the man right. It was much too tempting, that kind of money would allow him to spend two years traveling.

"The only thing we need is that you give us an answer as quickly as possible. Tomorrow, ideally. Please, call this public telephone at four in the afternoon."

Paulo grabbed the card extended before him; it had a number printed on it, perhaps because they had entered a period of large-scale distribution of goods, perhaps for fear someone might analyze the handwriting.

"I ask that you excuse me, but I need to get back to work. Many thanks for visiting my modest little office. All that I do is allow people to find happiness."

And with that, the man stood up, opened the door, and Paulo stepped out once again into the room where people lined the walls or lay across dirty mattresses scattered across the floor. He passed by the security guard, who this time gave him a knowing smile.

He walked out into the drizzle, asking God for help, to light the way, to not forsake him at that moment.

He was in a part of the city that was unfamiliar to him, he wasn't sure how to get back to the city center, he had no map, he had nothing. Of course a taxi would get the job done in an emergency, but he felt the need to walk through the drizzle, which soon transformed into a serious rain that didn't seem to wash much of anything clean—not the air around him, or his mind barraged with thoughts of those five thousand dollars.

He asked how he could get to Dam Square, but people walked right past him—one more crazy hippie who'd landed here and couldn't find his people. Finally, a Good Samaritan, a man at a newsstand laying out the next day's newspapers, sold him a map and showed him where to go.

He arrived back at the hostel, the night watchman lit his special lamp used for seeing if he had that day's stamp—the guests always received a stamp before leaving, made of some sort of invisible ink. No, he had the previous day's stamp, he'd just been through twenty-four hours that seemed never to end. He needed to pay for another night, but begged, "Please, don't stamp me now, I need to take a shower, I need to clean up, I'm dirty in every possible way."

The doorman consented and asked him to return in no more than a half hour because his shift was ending. Paulo walked into the mixed bathroom, everyone talking loudly, and then returned to his room, grabbed the paper with the telephone number that he'd carried all the way there, went back to the bathroom, already undressed, paper in hand. The first thing he did was to tear it into pieces, soak it so that he could never put it all back together, and then throw it on the floor. Someone complained—that was no place to be throwing things on the floor, he should use a trash can beneath one of the sinks. Others stopped to look at this animal who didn't know how to take care of the space around him, but he didn't meet their gaze or explain a thing—he simply obeyed as he hadn't obeyed anyone in a very long time.

After he did this he got back into the shower and felt reassured; now he was free. Of course, he could always return to the place he'd just come from and get the number again but he knew he would be barred, he'd had his chance and hadn't taken it.

Which left him feeling very happy.

He lay down on the bed—his demons had gone away, he was certain of it. The demons that expected him to accept their offer and bring them more subjects for their realm. He thought it was ridiculous to think that way—after all, drugs had already been demonized enough—but in this case people were right. It was truly ridiculous—he, who had always defended drugs as a sort of expansion of the consciousness, was now there hoping that Dutch police would put an end to their tolerance of these houses of the rising sun, arrest everybody, and send them far away from those who wanted only peace and love for the world.

He spoke to God, or an angel, because he could not sleep. He walked over to the closet where he'd put his stuff, took the key from his neck, grabbed a notebook where he often scribbled some thoughts and experiences. But he had no intention of reporting everything that Ted had told him—it was unlikely he would write about that in the future. He merely recorded the words that, so he imagined, God had spoken to him:

> There is no difference between the sea and the waves
> When a wave swells, it is made of water
> When it breaks against the sand, it is also made of the
>   same water.
> Tell me, Lord: Why are the two things the same? Where do
>   the mystery and the end lie?
> The Lord responds: Everything and everybody is the same;
>   this is the mystery and the end.

When Karla arrived, the Brazilian was already there—enormous bags under his eyes, as though he'd spent the entire night without sleeping, or as though . . . She preferred not to think about the second possibility, as this would imply he was someone she could never trust again, and she'd already grown used to his presence and his scent.

"So, let's go see a windmill, one of those Dutch icons?"

He slowly got up and began to follow her. They took a bus and eventually left Amsterdam behind them. Karla told him that it was necessary to buy a ticket—there was a machine inside the vehicle—but he preferred to ignore her warning; he'd slept poorly, was tired of everything, and needed to get his energy back. He felt his strength beginning to return.

The landscape was unchanging: immense plains, interrupted by dikes and drawbridges, where barges passed, carrying something somewhere. He couldn't see windmills in any direction, but it was day and the sun was shining again, provoking Karla to comment on just how rare that was—it was always raining in the Netherlands.

"I wrote something yesterday," Paulo said, taking a notebook from his pocket and reading aloud. She said neither that she liked it nor that she disliked it.

"Where is the sea?"

"The sea was here. There's an old proverb: *God created the world but the Dutch created the Netherlands*. But it's far from here—we can't see a windmill and the sea in a single day."

"No, I don't want to see the sea. Or even a windmill— something that, I imagine, must captivate tourists. That's not the kind of trip I'm on, as you must have realized by now."

"So why didn't you say anything back there? I'm tired of following the same old route to show my foreign friends something that doesn't even serve its original purpose anymore. We could have stayed in the city."

. . . And gone directly to the spot where they sell bus tickets, she thought. But she left that part out; she had to wait for the right moment to pounce.

"I didn't say anything back there because . . ."

. . . The story escaped from his mouth, it was beyond his control.

Karla stood listening, relieved and apprehensive at the same time. Was his reaction not a bit extreme? Was Paulo the type that swung between euphoria and depression and vice versa?

When he was done with his story, he felt better. The girl had listened quietly without judging him. She didn't seem to think that he had thrown five thousand dollars in the bathroom garbage. She didn't consider him weak—and that alone made him feel stronger.

They finally made it to the windmill, where a group of tourists was gathered listening to their guide: "the oldest example can be found in [unpronounceable name], the tallest in [unpronounceable name], they were used in the grinding of corn, coffee beans, cacao, the production of oil, and helped our explorers to transform large slats of wood into ships, and as a result, we went far, the empire expanded . . ."

Paulo heard the sound of a bus engine turning over, he grabbed Karla by the hand and begged to go back quickly to the city in the same vehicle on which they'd arrived. Two days from then, neither he nor the tourists would remember anything about the uses for a windmill. He hadn't come all that way to learn this sort of thing.

On the way back, during one of the stops, a woman got on, put on an armband that read TICKET COLLECTOR, and began to ask everyone for their ticket. When it was Paulo's turn, Karla looked away.

"I don't have one," he responded. "I thought the bus was free."

The ticket collector must have heard this sort of excuse a million times, because her response, which sounded rehearsed, was that Netherlands were very generous, no doubt, but only those with an exceptionally low IQ could think the country also had free transportation.

"Have you ever seen such a thing in any part of the world?"

Of course not, but he'd also never seen . . . Just then he felt Karla nudge him with her foot and he decided not to argue any further. He paid twenty times the value of the ticket, plus he was subjected to ugly looks from the other passengers—all of them Calvinists, honest, law-abiding folks, not one of whom had the air of someone who frequented Dam Square or its environs.

When they stepped off the bus, Paulo felt uncomfortable—was he trying to impose his presence on that girl who'd been so nice, though always determined to get what she wanted? Was it not time to say goodbye and let her carry on with her life? They barely knew one another and had already spent more than twenty-four hours together, joined at the hip, as though it were natural.

Karla must have read his mind because she invited him to go with her to the agency where she was going to buy her bus ticket to Nepal.

A bus ticket!

This was crazy beyond anything he could imagine.

The so-called agency was in fact a tiny office with a single employee, who introduced himself as Lars something or other, one of those names that was impossible to remember.

Karla asked when the next Magic Bus (that's what it was called) was scheduled to depart.

"Tomorrow. We only have two spots left and they're certain to be filled. If the two of you don't go, someone along the way will stop us and ask to get on."

Well, at least she wouldn't have enough time to change her mind . . .

"And it's not dangerous for a woman to travel alone?"

"I doubt you'll be alone for more than twenty-four hours. You'll have made it through all of the male passengers long

112

before you arrive in Kathmandu. You and the other women traveling alone."

How strange—Karla had *never* considered this possibility. She'd lost tons of time looking for a travel companion, a whole bunch of frightened little boys who were only prepared to explore what they already knew—for them, even Latin America must have posed a threat. They liked to pretend they were free as long as they were within safe range of their mothers' skirts. She noticed Paulo trying to hide his agitation, and this made her happy.

"I'd like a one-way ticket. I'll worry about the return later."

"To Kathmandu?"

This Magic Bus made several stops to pick up or drop off passengers—Munich, Athens, Istanbul, Belgrade, Tehran, or Baghdad (depending on which route was open).

"To Kathmandu."

"You sure you don't want to see India?"

Paulo could see that Karla and Lars were flirting. So what? She wasn't his girlfriend, she wasn't anything more than a recent acquaintance, kind but keeping her distance.

"How much to Kathmandu?"

"Seventy American dollars."

Seventy dollars to go to the other end of the world? What kind of bus was this? Paulo couldn't believe his ears.

Karla took the money from her belt and handed it to the "travel agent." This Lars filled out a receipt like those you get in restaurants, without any information beyond a person's name, passport number, and final destination. He then filled a section of the receipt with stamps that in reality meant nothing but lent an air of respectability to the whole operation. He handed it to Karla along with a map of the route.

"There are no refunds in the event of closed borders, natural disasters, armed conflicts along the way, that sort of thing."

She understood perfectly.

"When's the next Magic Bus?" Paulo asked, emerging from his silence and his brooding.

Lars's tone became slightly hostile. "It depends. We're not a regular bus line, as you might have guessed." He'd taken Paulo for an idiot.

"That I know, but you didn't answer my question."

"In theory, if everything's in order with Cortez's bus, he ought to get here in two weeks, rest for a bit, and then take off before the end of the month. But I can't promise anything—Cortez, like our other drivers . . ."

The way he said "our," it was almost as if he were referring to a large enterprise, something he'd denied being a short time before.

". . . gets tired of taking the same route all the time. They own the vehicles they drive, and Cortez could decide to go to Marrakech, for example. Or Kabul. He always talks about such things."

Karla said goodbye, but not before flashing a killer look at the Swede before her.

"If I weren't so busy, I'd offer to drive you myself," Lars said in response to Karla's wordless message. "That way we could get to know each other better."

As far as he was concerned, the girl's male companion didn't exist.

"There'll be a chance yet. When I make it back, we can grab a coffee and see how things develop."

It was at that moment that Lars, leaving behind the arrogant tone of someone who owned the world, said something no one was expecting.

"Those who go to the very end never come back—at least not for a good two or three years. That's what the drivers tell me."

Kidnappings? Muggings?

"No, none of that. The nickname for Kathmandu is 'Shangri-la,' the valley of paradise. Once you get used to the altitude, you're going to find everything you need there. And it's unlikely you'll ever want to come live in a city again."

As he handed her the ticket, he also handed her another map marked with all the stops.

"Tomorrow at eleven o'clock. Everyone here. Whoever doesn't make it doesn't get on."

"But isn't that too early?"

"You'll have plenty of time to sleep on the bus."

Karla, who was a stubborn and headstrong person, had decided the day before, when they'd met at Dam Square and walked around, that Paulo had to go with her. Though they'd spent little more than twenty-four hours together, she enjoyed his company. And she was comforted by the fact that she would never fall in love with him, because she was already feeling a bit strange about the Brazilian, and this needed to pass soon. As far as she was concerned, there was nothing better than to spend time with a person before their charm dissipated, in less than a week.

If things continued their current course and she left behind in Amsterdam the man she still considered her ideal, her trip would be completely ruined by the constant memory of him. And, if the image of this ideal man continued to grow in her mind, she would turn around halfway through her trip, they would end up marrying—something that was absolutely not in her plans for this incarnation—or he would set off for some distant, exotic land full of Indians and snakes slithering down the streets of its big cities (though she thought this second part could well be legend, like many other things people said about his country).

For her, Paulo was merely the right person at the right time. She had no plans to transform her trip to Nepal into a nightmare—constantly fending off other men's proposals. She was going because doing so seemed to her the craziest thing she could do, something far beyond her limits—she who had practically been raised without any limits at all.

She would never follow the Hare Krishna through the streets, she would never fall victim to one of the many Indian gurus she'd met who knew only how to teach people to "empty their minds." As though a mind that was empty, entirely empty, could bring someone closer to God. After her first frustrated experiences in that direction, the only thing left was direct communication with the Supreme Being, whom she feared and worshiped at the same time. The only things she cared about were solitude and beauty, direct communication with God, and above all a safe distance from the world that she already knew all too well and that no longer held any interest for her.

Wasn't she rather young to act like this, to think like this? She could always change her mind in the future, but as she'd said to Wilma in the coffee shop, paradise—as conceived by Westerners—was a trivial, monotonous, and dull place.

Paulo and Karla sat outside a café that served only coffee and biscuits—none of the products they'd managed to find in other coffee shops. They kept their faces turned to the sun—another sunny day, after the rain the day before—aware that this was a blessing that could vanish from one moment to the next. They hadn't exchanged a single word since leaving the "travel agency," the tiny office that had also caught Karla by surprise—she had expected something more professional.

"So . . ."

". . . So, today could be our last day together. You're headed east and I'm headed west . . ."

"Piccadilly Circus, where you're going to find a copy of what you saw here, the only difference being what you'll find in the middle of the square. No doubt the statue of Mercury is much more attractive than the phallic symbol here in Dam."

Karla didn't know it, but ever since her conversation at the "travel agency," Paulo had begun to feel an incredible desire to join her. More specifically, to see places one goes only once in a lifetime—and all for just seventy dollars. He refused to accept the idea that he was falling for the girl at his side, simply because it wasn't true, it was still just a possibility, he would never fall for someone who had no desire to return his love.

He began to study the map: they would cross the Alps, travel through at least two Communist countries, arrive in the first Muslim country he had ever been to in his life. He'd read so much about the dervishes who danced and whirled about as they opened themselves to the spirits, and at one point, he'd gone to see a group that had been visiting Brazil and had put on a show in his city's top theater. Everything that for so long had been only words on a page could now become reality.

For seventy dollars. In the company of people with his same adventurous spirit.

Yes, Piccadilly Circus was only a circular city square where people sat around in their bright clothes, where police went unarmed, the bars closed at eleven at night, and tours left to visit historic sites and such things.

A few minutes later he'd already changed his mind—an adventure is much more interesting than a city square. The ancients said that change is permanent and constant—because life passes quickly. If there was no change, there would be no universe.

Could he really change his mind so quickly?

Many are the emotions that move the human heart when it resolves to dedicate itself to the spiritual path. The reason could be noble—such as faith, brotherly love, or charity. Or it could merely be a whim, the fear of loneliness, a feeling of curiosity, or the desire to be loved.

None of this matters. The true spiritual journey is stronger than the reasons that lead us to it. It slowly begins to take hold, bringing love, discipline, and dignity. The moment arrives when we look back, we remember what we were like at the beginning of our journey, and we laugh at ourselves. We were capable of growing, even though our feet took to the road for reasons that we considered important but that were in fact quite futile. We were capable of changing direction at the moment this became crucial.

God's love is stronger than the reasons that lead us to Him. Paulo believed this with every fiber of his soul. God's power is with us at every moment, and courage is required to let it into our minds, our feelings, our breath—courage is required to change our minds when we realize that we are merely instruments of His will, and it is His will we ought to fulfill.

"I suppose you're waiting for me to say yes, because since yesterday, at Paradiso, you've carefully been laying your trap."

"You're crazy."

"Always."

Yes, she really did want him to come along with her, but like every woman who knows how men think, she couldn't say anything. Had she said something, he would have felt like a conqueror or worse, like the conquered. Paulo had caught on to the whole game—he'd even called it a trap.

"Answer my question: Do you want me to go?"

"I'm entirely indifferent to the matter."

Please come, she thought to herself. Not because you're an especially interesting man—to tell the truth the Swede at the "tourist agency" was much more assertive and determined. But because I feel better when I'm with you. I was proud of you when you decided to take my advice and ended up saving an enormous number of souls with your decision to not take heroin to Germany.

"Indifferent? You mean it's all the same to you?"

"That's right."

"And, in this case, if I get up right now and go back to the 'travel agency' and buy the last ticket, you won't feel either more or less happy?"

She looked at him and smiled. She hoped her smile would say it all—she would be very happy if Paulo were her travel companion—but she could not and would not put this into words.

"You buy the coffees," he said, standing up. "I already spent a fortune today with that fine."

Paulo had read her smile, her need to disguise her joy. For that reason she said the first thing that came to mind:

"Here women always split the check. We weren't raised to be your sex objects. And you were fined because you didn't listen to me. Okay what do I care if you listen, I'll pay the bill today."

What an annoying woman, Paulo thought. She has an opinion on everything—whereas in reality he loved the way she asserted her independence every second.

As they walked back to the agency, he asked her if she really thought they could make it to Nepal, a place so far away, on such a cheap ticket.

"A few months ago, I had my doubts, even after I saw the clipping announcing bus trips to India, Nepal, Afghanistan— always for around seventy to a hundred dollars. Until I read the story in *Ark,* an alternative newspaper, of someone who had gone and come back, and I felt I absolutely had to do it, too."

She left out the fact she was thinking about simply going, returning only after a few years. Paulo might not like the idea of coming back alone across the thousands of miles that separated them from their destination.

But he'd just have to figure it out—life is all about figuring it out.

There was nothing magic about the famous Magic Bus, which looked nothing like the posters she'd seen at the agency—a brightly colored vehicle full of drawings and messages. It was just a bus that at some point must have been used for taking children to school, with seats that didn't recline and a metal frame on top, where gallons of gasoline and extra tires were tied down.

The driver brought the group together—perhaps about twenty people in total, all of them looking like they'd stepped out of the same movie. They ranged from underage runaways (there were two such girls, and no one had asked them for identification) to an older man who kept his eyes locked on the horizon, with the look of someone who'd already reached a long-coveted enlightenment and had now decided to embark on a journey, a long journey.

There were two drivers: one who spoke with a British accent and the other who by all indications came from India.

"Though I hate rules, there are a few we'll need to follow. The first: no one can carry drugs across borders. In some countries this spells prison, but in others, such as those in Africa, it can spell death by decapitation. I hope you've all listened closely to what I've just told you."

The driver paused to gauge whether they'd understood. He suddenly seemed to have everyone's attention.

"Below, instead of baggage, I'm carrying gallons of water and army rations. Each ration contains beef puree, crackers, cereal bars with fruit filling, a chocolate bar with nuts or caramel, orange juice mix, sugar, salt. Be prepared for cold food for much of the trip after we cross into Turkey.

"Visas are granted at the borders: transit visas. They cost money, but nothing too expensive. Depending on the country, such as Bulgaria—which is under Communist rule—no one can jump off the bus. Take care of your bathroom needs before we leave, because I won't make any special stops."

The driver glanced at his watch.

"Time to go. Take your backpacks onto the bus with you— and I hope you've brought sleeping bags. We'll stop at night, sometimes at gas stations I know, but most of the time in the countryside, near the road. In some spots where neither option is possible—such as Istanbul—we know some cheap hotels."

"Could we not place our backpacks on top of the bus to leave more space for our legs?"

"Of course you can. But don't be surprised if they're not there when we stop for coffee. Inside, in the back of the bus, we have space for luggage. One piece, as it says on the back of the slip with a map of our route. And drinking water isn't included in the price of the ticket, so I hope you've brought your water bottles. You can always fill them up when we stop for gas."

"And if something goes wrong?"

"What do you mean?"

"If one of us gets sick, for example."

"I have a first aid kit. But as the name itself suggests, it's just *first aid*. Enough to make it to some city and leave any sick passengers there. So be sure to take care, very good care of your physical health, just like you like to think you do with your souls. I'm sure you all have been vaccinated against yellow fever and smallpox."

Paulo had the first vaccination—no Brazilian could leave his country without it, perhaps because foreigners always imagined them to be carrying all sorts of diseases. But he hadn't had the smallpox vaccine, since in Brazil it was believed that a childhood illness—measles—provided the body with natural immunity.

Whatever the case, the driver didn't ask anyone for a vaccination record. People began boarding and choosing their seats. More than one person set their backpacks on the seats next to them, but soon they were confiscated by the driver and thrown in back.

"Other people are going to board along the way, jerks."

The girls who looked to be underage, perhaps they were using fake passports, sat next to one another. Paulo sat next to Karla, and the first thing they did was work out a system of rotating shifts to see who would take the window. Karla suggested they trade places every three hours, and that at night, so they could get a decent night's sleep, she would sit next to the window. Paulo took this suggestion to be immoral and unjust since that would leave her with somewhere to rest her head. They agreed that they would alternate nights taking the window seat.

The engine turned over, and the school bus, with nothing romantic about it beyond its name, Magic Bus, began the journey of thousands of miles that would take them to the other side of the world.

"As the driver was talking, I got the feeling we were starting off not on some adventure but on some sort of mandatory military service, like we have in Brazil," Paulo said to his companion, remembering the promise he'd made to himself as he descended the Andes by bus and the many times he had broken it.

The comment irked Karla, but she couldn't start a fight or move places just five minutes into their journey. She took the book from her handbag and began to read.

"So, are you happy we're going to the place you wanted? By the way, the guy back at the 'agency' pulled one over on us—there are still empty seats."

"He didn't pull one over on us—you heard the driver say other people will climb on along the way. And I'm not going to the place I wanted—I'm returning to it."

Paulo couldn't make sense of her response, and she didn't provide any further explanation, so he decided to leave her in peace and began to concentrate on the broad flatlands around him, intersected by canals on all sides.

Why had God created the world and the Dutch, the Netherlands? Was there not much land on the planet waiting to be occupied?

Two hours later everyone had become friends—or had at least introduced themselves, since one group of Australians, though friendly and full of smiles, wasn't very interested in talking. Nor was Karla; she pretended to read that book whose name she'd already forgotten, but she must have been thinking about nothing but their destination, their arrival in the Himalayas, even though they were still thousands of miles away. Paulo knew from experience how such things could generate anxiety, but he didn't say a word; as long as she didn't take her bad mood out on him, everything was fine. If she did, he would change places.

Behind them were two French people, a father and his daughter, who seemed neurotic but enthusiastic. Next to them, an Irish couple; the young man introduced himself right away and took the opportunity to tell them he'd made the trip once before. Now, he was going back with his girlfriend because Kathmandu—"if we manage to make it there, of course"—was a place where you ought to spend at least two years. He'd come back earlier the first time because of his job, but now he'd left it all behind, sold his collection of miniature cars, had made a good bit of money with this (how could a miniature car collection render so much money?), and left his apartment. He summoned his girlfriend to go with him, and had a smile that stretched from one side of his face to the other.

Karla listened to the part about it being "a place where you ought to spend at least two years" and, abandoning the pretense she was reading, asked why.

Rayan, as the Irishman was called, explained that in Nepal he'd felt as if he'd stepped outside time, stepped into a parallel reality where everything was possible. Mirthe, Rayan's girlfriend, was neither friendly nor unfriendly, but she no doubt wasn't convinced that Nepal was a place everyone should spend the coming years.

However, by the looks of it, her love had won out.

"What do you mean, 'parallel reality'?"

"That spiritual state that takes over your body and soul when you feel happy, your heart filled with love. Suddenly, everything that's part of your daily life takes on a new meaning; colors become more vibrant, what bothered you before—like cold, rain, solitude, study, work—everything seems new. Because, for at least a fraction of a second, you've entered the soul of the universe and tasted the nectar of the gods."

The young Irishman seemed content to have to put into words something that could only be experienced. Mirthe looked as if she wasn't much liking this conversation with the pretty Dutch girl—she was entering the opposite parallel reality, the one that makes everything all of a sudden seem ugly and overwhelming.

"There's the other side, too, when the tiny details of our daily life transform into problems out of nothing," Rayan continued, as though guessing at his girlfriend's state of mind. "There is not one but many parallel realities. We're on this bus because that's what we've chosen; we have thousands of miles ahead of us and we can choose how we travel: in search of a dream that once seemed impossible or thinking about how the seats are uncomfortable and everyone's unbearable. Everything we envision now will set the tone for the rest of the trip."

Mirthe pretended not to understand that the comment was directed at her.

"When I was in Nepal for the first time, it seemed I had a sort of pact with Ireland, and this pact had not been broken. A voice in the back of my head kept repeating: 'Live this moment, make the most of each second because you're going to return to your country, don't forget to take photographs to show your friends how you were fearless and courageous and had experiences they would like to have but lack the courage to chase.'

"Until one day, I went to visit a cave in the Himalayas with a few other people. To our surprise, in a place where practically nothing grows, there was a tiny flower, half the size of a finger. We thought it was a miracle, a sign, and to show our respect we decided to hold hands and chant a mantra. A few seconds later the cave seemed to tremble, the cold no longer bothered us, the mountains in the distance suddenly seemed closer. And why did this happen? Because those who had lived there before left behind a love vibration that you could almost touch, that was capable of holding sway over anyone and anything that came to that place. Just like that flower seed the wind had carried there, as though desire—the enormous desire we all had that the world outside could be a better place—were taking on physical form and affecting everything in its path."

Mirthe must have heard that story several times, but Paulo and Karla were fascinated by Rayan's words.

"I don't know how long it lasted, but when we returned to the monastery where we were staying and recounted what had happened, one of the monks told us that someone who they referred to as a saint had lived there for decades. The monks also said that the world was changing and that all passions, absolutely all of them, would become more intense. Hate would grow stronger and more destructive, and love's face would shine through."

The driver interrupted the conversation, saying that, in theory, we ought to continue on to Luxembourg and spend the night but since he imagined that no one there had the goal of stopping in the principality, they would continue driving and sleep in the open air near a German city named Dortmund.

"I'm going to stop soon so we can grab something to eat and I'll call the office, letting them know the next passengers ought to be ready for an early departure. If no one is going to Luxembourg, we'll save precious miles."

Applause. Mirthe and Rayan were about to return to their seats when Karla interrupted them.

"But I thought you could only leap into a parallel reality by meditating and surrendering your heart to the Divine One?"

"I do this every day. But I also think about that cave every day. About the Himalayas. About those monks. I think I've done my time in what they call Western civilization. I'm looking for a new life. Not to mention, now that the world is in fact changing, both positive and negative emotions are going to gain force, and I—we, actually—am not about to face the dark side of life."

"There's no need," Mirthe said, taking part in the conversation for the first time and showing that she'd been able to overcome jealousy's venom in just a few minutes.

In some sense, Paulo knew everything that Rayan had just told them. He'd already had similar experiences—in most situations where he'd had a choice between revenge and love, he'd chosen love. It hadn't always been the right choice, at times he'd been called a coward, at times he himself was moved more by fear than by the sincere desire to make the world a better place. He was a human being, with all the fragility that entails; he didn't understand everything that happened in his life, but he truly wished to believe he was traveling in search of the light.

For the first time since he'd climbed onto the bus, he understood that it had been written, he needed to make that journey, to meet those people, to do something that he often preached but hadn't always had the courage to do: deliver himself up to the universe.

As time went on, people split off into groups, in some cases on account of language, in others because there was some nonverbal interest at play—sex, for example. For everyone but the two girls—most certainly minors, they kept a distance from everything and everybody precisely because they felt they were the center of attention, which they were not—the first five days had gone by quickly, because everyone was discovering themselves in the others and trading stories. Boredom was not a passenger, and the routine was broken only by stops at gas stations to fill up the gas tank and their water bottles, grab a sandwich and a drink, go to the bathroom. The rest was conversation, conversation, and more conversation.

Everyone slept beneath the stars, more times than not jittering with cold but grateful to be able to look to the sky and know that they could speak with the silence, sleep in the company of angels they could almost see, cease to exist for a few moments—even if it were only fractions of a second—as they felt eternity and infinity all around them.

Paulo and Karla paired off with Rayan and Mirthe—more accurately, Mirthe joined the group against her will; she'd already heard that story about parallel realities many times in her life. Her participation, meanwhile, was limited to keeping constant vigil over her man so that she didn't find herself forced to turn back midway because she hadn't managed to do something rather simple: continue being an interesting woman even after two years with Rayan.

Paulo had also noted interest on the part of the Irishman, who at the first opportunity asked whether he and Karla were together, receiving a direct response from Karla:

"No."

"Good friends, then?"

"Not even. Just travel companions."

And wasn't that the truth? Paulo decided to accept things as they were and forget pointless romanticism. They were two mariners sailing to some far-off land; though they shared a cabin, one slept on the bottom bunk and the other on top.

The more interest Rayan showed in Karla, the more Mirthe became insecure, her fury building—without her letting on, of course, because this would entail an unacceptable sign of submissiveness—and sidled up to Paulo, sitting next to him as they spoke and, now and then, resting her head on his shoulder as Rayan told them about everything he had learned after returning from Kathmandu.

"A mazing!"

After six days on the road, enthusiasm gave way to boredom and routine set in, permeating the atmosphere. Now that no one had anything new to say, everyone began to think about how they'd hardly done anything but eat, sleep outside, try to find a more comfortable position in their seats, open and close windows on account of cigarette smoke, grow tired of telling their own stories and talking with others— who never lost an opportunity to exchange little barbs here and there, like the rest of humanity did when in a herd, even if it was small and full of good intentions like this one.

That is, until the mountains emerged before them. And the valley. And the river that cut through the giant rocks. Someone asked where they were, and the Indian man from earlier said they had just crossed into Austria.

"Soon we'll get off and stop near the river running in the middle there so we can all clean up. Nothing better than cold water to make you feel that you have blood running in your veins and thoughts you can cast aside."

Everyone became excited by the idea of taking off all their clothes, the absolute freedom, this connection to nature without any intermediaries.

The driver turned onto a rocky road, the bus swung from one side to the other, and many people screamed for fear of turning over, but the driver only chuckled. They had finally arrived at the bank of a stream or, more accurately, a branch of the river that broke off from the rest, forming a gentle curve where the water was calmer before it rejoined the flowing current.

"Half an hour. Take the opportunity to wash what you're wearing."

Everyone ran for their backpacks—any hippie pack always included a tiny hand towel, a toothbrush, and bars of soap, since they always ended up camping rather than staying in hotels.

"It's so funny, this business of people thinking we don't take showers. It's possible we're even cleaner than the majority of all the family men and women who level these accusations."

Accusations? Who cared about that? Simply recognizing these criticisms gave power to their critics. The person who made this comment was the target of a series of angry looks—they had never paid any attention to what others said. Well, that was only half-true; they liked to call attention with their clothes and their flowers, their open and provocative sensuality, their low-cut blouses that hinted at breasts without bras, that sort of thing. And long skirts, because these were more sensual and more elegant—at least that was the determination of the group's self-proclaimed stylists, whoever they were. Sensuality, by the way, wasn't a means of attracting men but a way of being proud of your own body and making sure everyone noticed.

Those without towels grabbed spare T-shirts, blouses, sweaters, underwear—anything that could be used to dry off. Then they went down to the river, tossing off their clothing as they ran except the two young girls, of course, who took off their clothes but kept on their bras and panties.

A fairly strong cold wind blew in, and the driver explained that because the place they'd come to was dry and at a high altitude, the humidity and the air currents would help everything to dry much faster.

"That's why I picked this spot."

No one along the road above could see what was happening. The mountains kept the sun from coming out, but such was the place's beauty—rocks surrounded them on both sides, pine trees clinging to the sides, stones polished by centuries of friction—that the first thing they decided to do was to throw themselves into the cold water without thinking—all at once, shouting, throwing water on one another, a moment of communion among the varied groups that had formed, as though to say, "This is why we live as pilgrims, because we belong to a world that hates standing still."

If we stay quiet for an hour, we'll begin to hear God, Paulo thought to himself. But if we cry out with joy, God will also hear us and come down to bless us.

The driver and his assistant, who must have seen the nude bodies of young people unafraid to bare themselves a million times, left the group to take a bath and went to check the tire pressure and oil.

That was the first time Paulo had seen Karla naked, and he had to keep his jealousy in check. Her breasts were neither large nor small, they reminded him of the model they'd seen during the photo shoot back in Dam Square—but actually, she was much, much more beautiful.

But the real queen of them all was Mirthe, with her long legs and perfect proportions, a goddess who'd descended upon some valley in the middle of the Austrian Alps. She smiled when she noticed Paulo watching her, and he smiled back, knowing that it all added up to nothing more than a game to make Rayan jealous and prompt him to distance himself from his Dutch temptation. As we all know, a game with ulterior motives can still become a reality—and for a moment Paulo dreamed of it and decided that from there on out he was going to make a greater effort with the woman who—of her own free will—was becoming increasingly close to him.

The travelers washed their clothes. The two annoying little girls pretended not to see the group of more than twenty nude people standing right next to them, and soon they seemed to have hit upon some captivating subject of conversation. Paulo washed and squeezed out his shirt and underwear, thought about washing his pants and using the spare ones he always carried with him, but he thought it better to leave this for the next group bath—jeans were useful in any situation, but they took a long time to dry.

He noted what seemed to be a small chapel on top of one of the mountains and the scores in the vegetation carved by the intermittent rivers that must have run through there each spring when the snow melted. At that moment, they were streaks of sand.

The rest was absolute chaos, the chaos of black rocks mixed with other rocks, without any order, any attention to appearance—which made them especially beautiful. They weren't trying to do anything, not even to fall into order or arrangement so as to better resist nature's constant assault. They could have been there for millions of years or a mere two weeks. Signs near the entrance asked drivers to be wary of rockslides, which meant the mountains were still in the process of formation, they were living, the rocks sought each other out the way human beings do.

This chaos was beautiful, it was the font of life, it was how he imagined the universe beyond that place—and also within himself. It was a beauty that wasn't the fruit of comparisons, of prayers, or desires—simply a way of living a long life in the form of rocks, of pine trees that threatened to plummet from the mountains but which must have been there for years because they knew they were welcome there, pleasing in the eyes of the rocks, and each adored the other's company.

"Further up there's some sort of church or a chapel," someone said.

Yes, everyone had noticed it but they all thought it had been a personal discovery and now they knew it wasn't, and they silently asked themselves if someone lived there or if it had been abandoned years earlier, why it was painted white in a place where the rocks were black, how someone had managed to climb up there to build it in the first place. But anyway, there was the chapel, the only thing that differed from the surrounding primal chaos.

And there they all stood, gazing at the pines and the rocks, trying to determine the exact location where the surrounding mountains peaked, putting their clean clothes back on, and realizing, once again, that a bath was capable of curing many sorrows that refuse to budge from our minds.

The bus horn blew, it was time to resume their journey—something they'd forgotten about completely amid the beauty of that place.

By the look of it, Karla could be a bit obsessive with certain subjects.

"But how did you learn all this about parallel realities? It's one thing to have an epiphany, a revelation in some cave, but returning over these thousands of miles is something else entirely. It's not as if there's a single spot where spiritual experiences are possible—God is all around us."

"Yes, God is all around us. I always keep him close when I walk through the fields of Dooradoyle—the place where my family has lived for centuries—or when I go to watch the sea in Limerick."

They were sitting at a restaurant on the side of the road, near the border with Yugoslavia—where one of the great loves of Paulo's life had been born and raised. Until that moment no one—not even Paulo—had encountered any trouble with visas. However, because Yugoslavia was a Communist country, he now felt uneasy, though the driver had told everyone not to worry—unlike Bulgaria, Yugoslavia was outside the Iron Curtain. Mirthe was next to Paulo, Karla next to Rayan, and everyone maintained an air of "everything's all right," even knowing that a change of couples might well be approaching. Mirthe had already said she didn't intend to stay long in Nepal. Karla had claimed she was going there with the possibility of never returning.

Rayan continued.

"When I lived in Dooradoyle, a city the two of you should visit someday, though it rains quite a bit, I thought that I was destined to spend the rest of my days there, with my parents, who hadn't even been to Dublin to see the capital of their country. Or I'd be like my grandparents, who lived in the country, had never seen the sea, and thought Limerick was 'too big a city.' For years I did everything they asked: school, work at a minimarket, school, rugby—because the city had its own team that played hard though it never managed to qualify for the national league—go to Catholic church, because it was part of my country's culture and identity, unlike those who live in Northern Ireland.

"I was used to all this, and would set off on weekends to see the ocean. Even though I was a minor, I drank beer because I knew the pub owner, and I began getting used to the idea that this was my fate. After all, what's wrong with living a calm and easy life, looking at all those houses that'd probably been built by the same architect, going out now and then with a girl, going to the stables just outside the village and discovering sex—good or not, it was sex, there were orgasms, though I was afraid to go all the way and end up punished by my parents or by God.

"In adventure books everyone follows their dreams, they go to incredible lands, pass through some adverse circumstances, but they always come back victorious to tell their battle stories at the market, at the theater, in films—in short, in all the places where there's someone to listen. We read these books and we think: my fate will be similar, I'll conquer the world in the end, I'll become rich, return to my country as a hero and everyone will envy me, respect me for what I've done. The women will smile as I walk by, the men will doff their hats and ask me to tell them for the thousandth time what happened in this or that situation, how I was able to take advantage of the only opportunity I had in my entire life and transform it into millions and millions of dollars. But these things only happen in adventure books."

The Indian (or Arab) man, who took turns at the wheel with the primary driver, came and sat next to them. Rayan continued his story.

"I went and served in the army, like the bulk of the boys in my city. Paulo, how old are you?"

"Twenty-three. But I didn't serve, I received a deferment because my father managed to get something we call third rank, in other words, reservist for the reservists, and now I can spend this time traveling. I think it's been two hundred years since Brazil fought a war."

"I served," said the Indian man. "Ever since we got our independence, my country has been at war—an undeclared war—with its neighbor. It's all the fault of the English."

"The English are always to blame," Rayan seconded. "They still occupy the northern part of my country, and just last year, right around the time I had returned from a paradise called

Nepal, things got worse. Now Ireland is at the brink of war after confrontations between Catholics and Protestants. They're sending troops in."

"Carry on with your other story," Karla interrupted. "How did you end up going to Nepal?"

"Bad influences," Mirthe interjected, laughing. Rayan also laughed.

"You're absolutely right. My generation grew up and my school friends began to move to America, where the Irish community is enormous and everyone has an uncle, a friend, some family."

"You're not going to tell me this is also the fault of the English."

"This is also the fault of the English," Mirthe said; it was her turn to enter the conversation. "They tried to starve our people to death twice. The second time, in the nineteenth century, they planted a fungus in our potato fields—our main source of sustenance—and the population began to wane. They estimate an eighth of the population died of hunger—*hunger!*—and two million had to leave the country in search of food. Thank God America received us with open arms yet another time."

That girl, who looked like a diva from some other planet, began to hold court on the subject of the two great famines, something Paulo had never heard of. Thousands dead, no one to support the people, a fight for independence, or things like that.

"I earned my degree in history," she said. Karla tried to guide the conversation back to what mattered—Nepal and parallel realities—but Mirthe didn't stop until she was finished teaching everyone how much Ireland had suffered, how many hundreds of thousands of people had starved to death, how the country's great revolutionaries went before the firing squad after two attempted uprisings, how finally an American (yes, an American!) forged a peace treaty for a war that had seemed it would never end.

"But this will never happen—never happen—again. Our resistance is much stronger now. We have the IRA and we're going to take the war to their land, with bombs, killings, whatever's possible. Sooner or later, as soon as they find a good excuse, they're going to have to march their dirty boots straight off of our island." And, turning to the Indian man: "Like they did in your country."

The Indian man—whose name was Rahul—had begun to tell what had happened in his country, but this time Karla adopted a stronger, more decisive tone.

"Shall we let Rayan finish his story?"

"Mirthe is right: it was 'bad influences' that led me to Nepal the first time. When I was serving in the army, I was in the habit of going to a pub in Limerick, near the barracks. They had everything there, darts, pool, arm wrestling, everyone trying to prove to the others how manly they were, how they were ready for any challenge. One of the regulars was an Asian guy who never spoke; all he ever did was drink two or three glasses of our national treasure—a dark beer called Guinness—and leave before the bar owner would ring the bell advising it was nearing eleven at night and the bar was about to close."

"It's all the fault of the English."

In fact, the tradition of closing at eleven had been set by Great Britain at the start of the war, as a means of keeping drunk pilots from setting off to attack Germany, or soldiers lacking discipline from waking up late, ruining morale.

"One fine day, tired of listening to the same stories of how everyone was getting ready to go to America as soon as they could, I asked permission to sit at the table of this Asian man. We sat there for maybe a half hour—I figured he might not speak English and I didn't want to make him self-conscious. But before leaving that day, he said something that stuck in my head: 'You may be here, but your soul is in another place—my country. Go in search of your soul.'

"I agreed and raised my glass to salute him, but avoided getting into details. My rigid Catholic upbringing kept me from imagining any scenario beyond body and soul united, awaiting their meeting with Christ after death. They are obsessed with this idea of the soul in the East, I told myself."

"Yes, we are," said Rahul.

Rayan realized he'd offended the man and decided to poke fun at himself.

"We're worse still, we think the body of Christ can be found in a piece of bread. Don't take me the wrong way."

The other man waved his hand, as if to say, "It's no big deal," and Rayan was finally able to finish his story—but only a part, because soon they would all be interrupted by some bad energy.

"So anyway, I was already resigned to return to my village, take care of our business—more specifically, my father's dairy farm—while the rest of my friends crossed the Atlantic to see the Statue of Liberty as it welcomed them, but I couldn't get that man's comment out of my head that night. The truth was I was trying to convince myself everything was all right, that I was going to find a girl one day and get married, have kids, far from this world of smoking and swearing where I lived, even though I'd never made it further than the cities of Limerick and Dooradoyle. I'd never been curious enough even to stop and have a walk through one of the small towns—villages, actually—between these two cities.

"At that time, I thought it was enough, safer and cheaper, to travel through books and films—no one on the planet had laid eyes on fields as beautiful as those that surrounded me. Still, I returned the next day to the pub, sat at the solitary man's table, and even knowing it's risky to ask questions that have a high probability of getting an answer, I asked him what he'd meant. Where was this country of his?"

Nepal.

"Anyone who's made it to high school has heard of a place called Nepal, but he's probably already learned and forgotten the name of its capital, the only thing he can remember is that it's far away. Maybe in South America, in Australia, in Africa, in Asia, but one thing's for certain, it's not in Europe, or else he would have met someone from there, seen a film, or read a book about it.

"I asked him what he'd meant the day before. He wanted to know what he'd told me—he couldn't remember. After I reminded him, he sat there staring at his glass of Guinness for several moments without saying anything, then finally he broke his silence: 'If I said that, perhaps you really ought to go to Nepal.' 'And how do you suppose I get there?' 'The same way I came here: by bus.'

"Then he left. The next day, when I asked to sit at his table so he could tell me more about this story of my soul awaiting me so far away, he told me he preferred to drink alone, as he did, after all, every night.

"Now, if it were a place I could reach by bus and I managed to find some company for the trip, who knows, maybe I would end up visiting that country after all.

"That's when I met Mirthe, in Limerick, sitting in the same spot I often visited to stare at the sea. I thought she wouldn't have any interest in some kid from the country whose destiny wasn't Trinity College in Dublin—where she was finishing her studies—but the O'Connell Dairy, in Dooradoyle. But we had an immediate connection, and during one of our conversations I told her about the unusual character from Nepal and what he'd said to me. Soon I would be going home for good and all that— Mirthe, the pub, my friends in the barracks, everything—would merely be a phase from my youth. I was caught by Mirthe's tenderness, her intelligence, and—why not just say it?—her beauty. If she thought I was deserving of her company, it would make me more secure, more confident in myself in the future.

"One long weekend, just before the end of my military service, she took me to Dublin. I saw the place where the author of *Dracula* had lived and Trinity College, where she studied, which was bigger than anything I could have dreamed. In one of the pubs near the university, we sat drinking until the owner rang the closing bell. I sat looking at the walls covered in photos of the writers who had made history in our land—James Joyce, Oscar Wilde, Jonathan Swift, William Butler Yeats, Samuel Beckett, George Bernard Shaw. At the end of our conversation, she handed me a piece of paper telling me how to get to Kathmandu. There was a bus leaving every fifteen days from the Totteridge and Whetstone subway station.

"I thought she'd grown tired of me, wanted me far, far away, and I grabbed the piece of paper without the slightest intention of going to London."

In the midst of telling his story, Rayan pretended not to hear a group of motorcycles pull up and then rev their engines in neutral. From the travelers' vantage point inside the restaurant, they couldn't tell how many bikers there were, but the sound was threatening and out of place. The manager of the restaurant mentioned they were closing soon, but no one at any of the other tables had budged and Rayan continued speaking.

"Then Mirthe surprised me with what she said: 'Setting aside travel time, which I won't mention so as not to discourage you, I want you to come back from there after exactly two weeks. I'll be here waiting for you—but if you aren't here by the day I think you ought to arrive, you'll never see me again.'"

Mirthe laughed. That wasn't exactly what she'd said—it was closer to "Go in search of your soul, because I've already found mine." What she hadn't said that day, and wasn't about to now, was "You are my soul. I'll pray every night that you return safely, that we meet again, and that you never want to leave my side, because you deserve me and I deserve you."

"Was she really going to wait for me? Me, the future owner of O'Connell Dairy Milk? What would she care for a kid with so little culture and so little experience? Why was it so important for me to follow the advice of some strange man I met in a pub?

"But Mirthe knew what she was doing. Because the moment I stepped onto that bus, after having read everything I could find about Nepal and then lying to my parents that the army had extended my service time for misconduct and was sending me to one of its most remote bases, in the Himalayas, I came back another person. I left as a hayseed, I came back as a man. Mirthe came to meet me, we slept in her house, and ever since we've never been apart."

"That's the problem," she said, and everyone at the table knew she was being sincere. "Of course I don't want some idiot at my side, but I also wasn't expecting someone who would say to me, 'Now it's your turn to go back with me.'"

She laughed.

"And what's worse, I accepted!"

Paulo was already feeling awkward about sitting next to Mirthe, their legs touching and, now and then, her hand rubbing his. The look in Karla's eyes was no longer the same—this wasn't the man she was looking for.

"Now what, do we talk about parallel realities?"

But the restaurant had filled with five people dressed in black, heads shaved, chains around their waists, tattoos in the form of swords and ninja stars, who had walked over to the table and surrounded the group without a word.

"Here's your bill," said the restaurant manager.

"But we haven't even finished eating," Rayan protested. "And we didn't ask for the bill."

"I did," said one of the members of the group that had just arrived.

The Indian man started to get up, but someone pushed him back down into the chair.

"Before you leave, Adolf wants you to promise never to come back. We hate freeloaders. Our people like law and order. Order and law. Foreigners aren't welcome here. Go back to wherever you came from with your drugs and your free love."

Foreigners? Drugs? Free love?

"We'll leave when we've finished eating."

Paulo was annoyed at Karla's comment—why provoke them further? He knew they were surrounded by people who truly hated everything they represented. The chains hanging from their pants, the motorcycle gloves with their metal appliqués of a much different variety from those he'd bought in Amsterdam. Tiny spikes designed to intimidate, to wound, to inflict serious harm when they decided to throw a punch.

Rayan turned around to face the one who appeared to be the boss—an older man, with wrinkles on his face, who'd looked on silently.

"We're from different tribes, but we're tribes that fight against the same thing. We'll finish and leave. We're not your enemies."

The boss, it appeared, had difficulty talking, since he stuck an amplifier to his neck before responding.

"We don't belong to any tribe" came the voice of the metallic instrument. "Get out of here now."

It seemed as if the next moment would never end, as the women looked the strangers in the eyes, the men weighed their options, and those who had just arrived waited in silence, except for one person who turned to the restaurant owner and screamed.

"Disinfect these chairs once they've left. They must have brought the plague with them, venereal disease, who knows what else."

The rest of the people there seemed not to pay any attention to what was happening. Perhaps one of them had summoned the group, someone who took the simple fact that there are free people in the world as a personal affront.

"Get out of here, you cowards," said someone else who had just arrived, a man with a skull stitched into his leather jacket. "Head straight and in less than a mile you'll find a Communist country where you'll no doubt be welcome. Don't come around here with your bad influence on our sisters and our families. We're Christians, our government doesn't allow trouble, and we respect others. Stick your tails between your legs and get out of here."

Rayan flushed red. The Indian man seemed indifferent, perhaps because he'd watched scenes like this before, perhaps because Krishna taught that no one should flee when he finds himself before the battlefield. Karla shot a look at the men with their shaved heads, especially the one to whom she'd remarked that they weren't done eating. She must have been bloodthirsty now that she'd discovered the bus trip was less interesting than she'd imagined.

It was Mirthe who grabbed her purse, took out what she owed, and calmly placed it on the table. Then, she walked to the door. One of the men barred her; once again there was a confrontation that no one wanted to see turn into a fight, but she pushed him—without politeness and without fear—and continued on her way.

The others got up, paid their portions of the bill, and left—which, in theory, meant they truly were cowards, capable of facing a long journey to Nepal but only too eager to run at the first sign of any real threat. The only one who seemed ready to take the group on was Rayan, but Rahul grabbed him by the shoulders and dragged him out, while one of the men with the shaved heads stood by opening and closing his penknife.

The two French travelers, father and daughter, also got up, paid their bill, and left with the others.

"You can stay, sir," the boss told him in the amplifier's metallic voice.

"I can't, actually. I'm with them, and it's a disgrace what's going on here, in a free country, with beautiful landscapes. The ultimate impression we're going to have of Austria is still the river splitting the rocks, the Alps, the beauty of Vienna, the magnificent Melk Abbey. A group of no-good . . ."

His daughter grabbed him by the arm as he continued talking.

". . . who don't represent this country will be promptly forgotten. We didn't come all the way from France for this."

Another man came from behind and punched the Frenchman in the back. The British bus driver stood between the two with eyes like steel—he stared at the boss without saying a word; there was no need, because his presence at that moment seemed to fill everyone with fear. The Frenchman's daughter began to scream. Those who were at the door began to turn back, but Rahul stopped them. The battle had been lost.

He walked back in, grabbed father and daughter by the arms,

and pushed them all out the door. They walked toward the bus. The driver was the last to leave. He didn't take his eyes off the leader of that gang of thugs, he showed no fear.

"Let's get out of here, go back a few miles, and sleep in some other town."

"And run away from them? Is that what we've come all the way here for, to run at the first sign of a fight?"

The older man had spoken up. The young girls looked petrified.

"That's right. Let's run," said the driver as the bus pulled forward. "I've already run from all sorts of things the few times I've taken this journey. I don't see any cause for shame in that. Worse would be if we woke up tomorrow with the tires slashed, unable to continue our journey because I only have two spares."

They made it to the town. They parked on a tranquil-looking street. Everyone was tense and shook up from the episode back at the restaurant; but now they were a group, capable of fending off any act of aggression. Still, they decided to sleep inside the bus.

They tried, making a great effort, to fall asleep, but two hours later bright lights began to illuminate the interior of the vehicle.

POLIZEI.

One of the policemen opened the door and said something. Karla spoke German and explained to everyone that they were to leave their stuff behind and step off the bus, wearing only the clothing on their body. At that time of night the air was freezing, but the police—men and women—refused to let them grab anything. They stood trembling with cold and fear, but no one seemed to care.

The police entered the vehicle, opened bags, backpacks—emptied everything onto the floor. They discovered a water pipe, generally used for smoking hashish.

The object was confiscated.

They asked everyone for their passports. They examined them carefully with their flashlights, saw the entry stamps, studied each page for a sign they were falsified—they would first shine their flashlights on a person's passport photo and then on his face. When they came to the "adult" girls, one of the policemen went to his car and radioed somewhere. He waited awhile, nodded, and then walked back to the two girls.

Karla translated.

"We have to take you to the office of child services, and your parents will be coming soon. Soon, well, perhaps two days or perhaps a week, depending on whether they can find plane or bus tickets—or rent a car."

The girls were in shock. One of them began to cry, but the policewoman carried on in her monotone voice:

"I don't know what you're trying to do and I don't care. But you're not going any further. I'm amazed you've made it across so many borders without anyone noticing you'd run away from home."

She turned to the driver.

"Your bus could be impounded for parking illegally. The only reason I'm not going to do that is because I want to see you gone as soon as possible, as far away as possible. Didn't you notice right away they were underage?"

"I noticed their passports said something else, different from what you're suggesting now, ma'am."

The policewoman was about to continue, explaining how the girls had forged documents, that you could *see* they were underage, that they'd run away from home because one of them claimed that in Nepal they could find much better hashish than what they had in Scotland—at least that's what was written in the file that had been read back through the radio. Their parents were desperate. But she decided to leave the conversation there, the only people she needed to explain herself to were her superiors.

The police confiscated the girls' passports and asked the girls to follow them. The girls started to protest, but the policewoman in charge didn't pay them any mind—neither of them spoke German, and the other police, though they likely knew English, refused to speak any other language.

The policewoman boarded the bus with the two girls and asked them to gather their stuff from the mess, which took some time while everyone else stood freezing outside. Finally, the two girls came out and were taken to a police car.

"Get a move on," said a lieutenant who had been keeping an eye on the group.

"If you haven't found anything, why should we go anywhere?" the driver asked. "Is there a place we can find to park without fear of having the vehicle impounded?"

"There's a field close by, just before you enter the city; you can sleep there. But you'd best be out of here when the sun comes up. We don't want to be disturbed with the sight of people like you."

The travelers lined up to grab their passports and then filed back onto the bus. The driver and his backup, Rahul, didn't move.

"And what was our crime? Why can't we spend the night here?"

"I've no obligation to answer your question. But if you prefer, I can take all of you in to the station, where we'll need to get in contact with your home countries while you wait in a cell without any heat. We have no trouble doing so. You, sir, could be accused of kidnapping minors."

One of the police cars pulled away with the girls inside, and no one on the bus ever discovered what they'd been doing there.

The lieutenant stared at the driver, the driver stared at the lieutenant, Rahul stared at them both. Finally, the driver gave in, climbed onto the bus, and started off again.

The lieutenant waved goodbye with a smirk on his face. These people didn't even deserve to be free, traveling from one side of the world to the other, spreading the seed of rebellion. It was enough that the events of May 1968 had happened in France—that had to be contained at all costs.

Sure, May 1968 had nothing to do with the hippies and those like them, but people were capable of confusing things and then trying to put an end to it all no matter where.

Would he like to join them? Absolutely not. He had a family, a house, kids, food, friends on the police force. As if it weren't enough to be so close to the border of a Communist country—someone had written once in the newspaper that the Soviets had changed tactics and were now using people to corrupt traditional values and turn them against their own governments. He thought that was a bit crazy, it made no sense, but he preferred not to run risks.

Everyone was talking about the insanity they'd just been through, except for Paulo, who seemed to have lost his ability to speak and had changed color. Karla asked whether he was all right—there was no way she was going to travel with someone who cowered at the first sign of the police— and he responded he was perfectly fine, he'd just had too much to drink and was feeling sick. When the bus stopped at the field the guard had mentioned, Paulo was the first to get off and vomit on the side of the road, hidden from sight, without anyone noticing. Only he knew about the things he had been through, his past in Ponta Grossa, the terror that seized him each time he reached a border crossing. And what was worse, the terror of knowing that his fate, his body, his soul, would forever be tied to the word "police." He would never feel safe. He'd been innocent when they locked him up and tortured him. He had never committed any crime except, perhaps, engaging in the sporadic use of drugs, which, by the way, he never carried on his person, even in Amsterdam, where there would be absolutely no consequences for doing so.

In the end, his imprisonment and torture were behind him in the physical sense but continued as present as ever in some parallel reality, in one of the many lives he lived all at once.

He sat far away from everyone and wanted nothing more than silence and solitude, but Rahul walked up to him with what looked like some sort of cold white tea. Paulo drank it—it tasted like expired yogurt.

"It won't be long before you feel better. Just don't lie down or try to sleep right now. And don't worry about explanations—some bodies are more sensitive than others."

They sat there for a while without moving. The substance began to take effect after fifteen minutes. Paulo stood up to join the group, which had lit a bonfire and was dancing around to the sound of the bus radio. They danced to exorcise their demons, they danced to show that, whether they wanted to be or not, they were stronger now.

"Stay a little longer," Rahul said. "Perhaps we ought to pray together."

"I must have got food poisoning," Paulo ventured.

But he could tell by the look on Rahul's face that he wasn't buying it. Paulo sat down again, and the man sat down in front of him.

"Let's say you're a warrior on the front line and suddenly the Enlightened Lord comes to observe the battle. Let's say your name is Arjuna, and he asks you not to back down, to soldier on and fulfill your destiny, because no one can kill or die, time is eternal. It just so happens that you, who are human, already went through a similar situation in one of your previous trips through the wheel of time and see the situation repeating itself— even though it's different, the emotions are the same. Remind me your name again?"

"Paulo."

"Okay, Paulo, you're not Arjuna, the all-powerful general who feared wounding his enemies because he was a good man, and Krishna didn't like what he was hearing because Arjuna was granting himself power that wasn't his to take. You are Paulo, you come from a distant country, you have moments of bravery and moments of cowardice, as we all do. In moments of cowardice you're gripped by fear.

"And fear, contrary to what most people say, has its roots in the past. There are gurus in my country who claim: 'Each time you take a step forward, you will feel fear at what you'll find.' But how can I fear what I'll find if I haven't already experienced pain, separation, internal and external torture?

"Do you remember your first love? It came in through a door full of light and you let it take over everything, to bring light to your life, fill your dreams, until, as always happens with our first love, one day it went away. You must have been seven or eight, she was a pretty girl your age, she found herself an older boyfriend, and there you were, suffering, telling yourself you would never love again—because loving is losing.

"But you loved again—it's impossible to conceive of a life without this feeling. And you continued to love and lose until you found someone . . ."

Paulo couldn't help but think that the next day they would enter the country of one of the many people to whom he had opened his heart, with whom he had fallen in love, and—once again—whom he had lost. She who had taught him so many things, including how to put on a brave face in moments of desperation. It truly was the wheel of fortune spinning in circular space, taking away good things and doling out pain, taking away pain and bringing other good things.

Karla kept one eye on the two men talking and another on Mirthe so that she wouldn't come close. The men were taking quite some time. Why hadn't Paulo come back and danced a bit around the bonfire, leaving behind the awful vibe that had taken root in the restaurant and followed them to the tiny city where they'd parked the bus?

She decided to dance a little more, while the sparks from the fire filled the starless sky with light.

The music was the domain of the bus driver, who was also recovering from that night's events—though this wasn't the first time he'd been through something like that. The louder the music and the more it was suited to dancing, the better. He considered the possibility that the police might show up again and ask him to leave, but he decided to relax. He wasn't about to live in fear because a group of people who considered themselves the ultimate authority, and, as a result, authorities over others, had tried to ruin a day in his life. It was all right, it was just one day, but one day was the most precious good he had on this earth. Just one day—his mother had begged on her death-bed. Just one day was worth more than all the kingdoms in the world.

Michael—this was the driver's name—had done something unthinkable three years earlier; after earning his medical degree, he'd received a used Volkswagen from his parents and, instead of parading it in front of the girls or flashing it before his friends in Edinburgh, he set off one week later on a trip to South Africa. He had saved enough to spend two or three years traveling—working in private clinics as a paid internist. His dream was to see the world, because he had become all too familiar with the human body; he had seen its fragility.

After countless days—spent crossing several former French and English colonies, treating the sick and consoling the afflicted—he got used to the idea that death was always near and promised himself that never, at any moment, would he allow the poor to suffer or the forgotten to live in discomfort. He discovered that charity had an effect that was both redemptive and sheltering—never, not even for an instant, had he faced adversity or gone hungry. The Volkswagen, which was already twelve years old, hadn't been built for this; but it held up, apart from a blown tire as he crossed one of those many countries in a constant state of war. Without his realizing it, the good that Michael did now preceded him wherever he went, and in each village, he was hailed as a man who saved lives.

By mere chance, he found a Red Cross outpost in a beautiful village near a lake in the Congo. There, his fame also preceded him—they supplied him with vaccines for yellow fever, bandages, this or that for performing surgeries, and they gave strict orders that he not get involved in the conflict but merely care for the wounded from both sides. "This is our goal," explained a young man from the Red Cross. "Not to interfere, merely to heal."

The trip Michael had intended to last two months stretched to nearly a year. Traveling miles, he was almost never alone and often transported women who could no longer walk after so many days on the road seeking refuge from the violence and tribal wars on every side. As he crossed through the countless checkpoints, he felt that a mysterious force was helping him. Soon after asking for his passport, they let him continue, perhaps for having healed a brother, a son, a friend of a friend.

That had impressed him a great deal. He'd made a vow to God—he asked to live each day as a servant, one day, a *single day,* in the image of Christ, to whom he was entirely devoted. He thought about becoming a priest as soon as he got to the other end of the African continent.

When he arrived in Cape Town, he decided to rest before seeking out a religious order and putting himself forward as an apprentice. His idol was Saint Ignatius of Loyola, who had followed a course much like his own, traveling part of the world and founding the Jesuit order after going to study in Paris.

Michael found a simple, cheap hotel and decided to rest for a week, to allow all the adrenaline to leave his body and peace to overtake him once again. He tried not to think about what he had seen—revisiting the past is no use, it serves only to place figurative shackles on our feet and remove any sign of hope in humanity.

He turned his attention to the future, thought about how to sell his Volkswagen, and spent morning to night admiring the view of the sea from his window. He watched as the colors of the sun and water changed according to the hour, and below, the white men wearing explorers' hats strolled along the beach, smoking pipes, their wives dressed as though they were at the royal court in London. Not a single black person, only whites there below, on the sidewalk that ran along the shore. This filled him with more sadness than you can imagine; racial segregation was the law in the country but at the moment he could do nothing, only pray.

He prayed morning to night, asking for inspiration, preparing himself to undertake Saint Ignatius's spiritual exercises for the tenth time. He wanted to be ready when the moment arrived.

On his third morning there, as he ate breakfast, two men in light suits approached his table.

"So, you're the man who has brought such honor to the name of the British Empire," one of them said to him.

The British Empire had ceased to exist, it had been replaced by the Commonwealth, but he had been caught off guard by the man's words.

"I've honored only one day at a time," he responded, knowing they wouldn't understand.

And, in fact, they didn't understand, because their conversation took the most dangerous direction he could have imagined.

"You're well liked and respected wherever you go. The British government needs people like you."

Had the man not mentioned the "British government," Michael would have thought he was being invited to work in the mines, plantations, mineral-processing plants, as a foreman or even as a doctor. But "British government" meant something else. Michael was a good man, but he wasn't naïve.

"No, thank you. I have other plans."

"Such as?"

"Becoming a priest. Serving God."

"And don't you think you would be serving God by serving your country?"

Michael understood he could no longer stay in the place he'd struggled so long to reach. He ought to return to Scotland on the next flight—he had the money.

He got up from his table without allowing the man a chance to continue the conversation. He knew what they were so kindly "inviting" him to do: become a spy.

He had good relations with the local tribal armies, he'd met many people, and the last—the very last—thing he was going to do was betray the confidence of those who trusted him.

He grabbed his things, spoke with the manager about selling his car, and gave the address of a friend to whom the money could be sent. He went to the airport and, eleven hours later, stepped off a plane in London. Reading the board of classified ads as he waited on the train that would take him into the city, he found one in particular among the postings for cleaning ladies, roommates, waitresses, and girls interested in working the cabaret bars. "Wanted: Drivers Willing to Go to Asia." Before heading into the city, he tore the announcement from the wall and went directly to the address listed, a tiny office with a sign on the door: BUDGET BUS.

"The position has been filled," he was told by a young man with long hair, who opened the window to allow the smell of hashish to filter out. "But I heard they're looking for qualified candidates in Amsterdam. Do you have experience?"

"Quite a bit."

"So go there. Tell them Theo sent you. They know me."

He handed Michael a piece of paper, with a more spirited name than Budget Bus: Magic Bus.

See countries you never thought you'd set foot in. Price: seventy dollars per person—travel only. The rest you bring with you—except drugs, or you'll have your throat slit before making it to Syria.

There was a photo of a bus painted in wild colors, a line of people standing before it, flashing the peace sign, the symbol of Churchill and of the hippies. He went to Amsterdam, and they hired him on the spot—it seemed demand was greater than the supply.

This was his third trip, and he never tired of crossing the gorges of Asia. He changed the music, putting on a cassette tape with a song list he had compiled himself. The first song was by

Dalida, an Egyptian singer living in France who was a hit across all of Europe. The passengers' mood lifted—the nightmare was over.

Rahul noticed that his Brazilian friend had made a full recovery.

"I saw how you faced down that group of thugs in black without much fear. You were ready to fight, but that would have presented a problem for us—we're pilgrims, not the owners of this earth. We rely upon the hospitality of others."

Paulo nodded.

"And yet, when the police showed up you froze. Are you running from something? Did you kill someone?"

"Never, but, if I'd been able a few years ago, I would have done it for sure. The problem is I could never see the faces of my potential victims."

In broad strokes, to keep Rahul from thinking he was lying, he told the story of what had happened in Ponta Grossa. The Indian man didn't show any particular interest.

"Ah, so you have a fear that's much more common than you think: the police. Everyone's afraid of the police, even those who spent their whole lives obeying the law."

This remark helped Paulo relax. He caught sight of Karla approaching.

"Why aren't you two with the rest of us? Now that the girls aren't with us, you've decided to take their place?"

"We're getting ready to pray, that's all."

"Can I pray with you?"

"Your dancing is already a form of praising God. Go back to the others and continue what you're doing."

But Karla, the second most beautiful woman on the bus, wasn't about to give up. She wanted to pray as Brazilians prayed. As far as Indians were concerned, she'd already seen them pray several times in Amsterdam, with their unusual postures, the dots between their eyes, that aura as though they were peering into infinity.

Paulo suggested they all join hands. As she was preparing to recite the first verse of a prayer, Rahul interrupted.

"Let's leave this spoken prayer for another time. Today, it's better we pray with the body—let's dance."

He walked back to the bonfire, and the other two followed him—everyone there saw dance and music as means to free themselves from their bodies. Of saying to themselves: "Tonight, we're together and happy, despite the efforts of the forces of evil to keep us apart. We're here, together, and we will continue on together along the road before us, though the forces of darkness seek to block our passage.

"Today, we gather here together, and one day, sooner or later, we must say goodbye. Despite not knowing one another properly, despite not having traded words we might have traded, we're here together for some mysterious motive we don't understand. This is the first time that the group has danced around a bonfire as the ancients did at a time when they were closer to the universe and watched the clouds and the storms, the fire and the wind move in harmony across the starry sky and decided to dance—to celebrate life.

"Dancing transforms everything, demands everything, and judges no one. Those who are free dance, even if they find themselves in a cell or a wheelchair, because dancing is not the mere repetition of certain movements, it's a conversation with a Being greater and more powerful than everyone and everything. To dance is to use a language beyond selfishness and fear."

And, that night, in September 1970, after being expelled from a bar and humiliated by the police, the people there danced and gave thanks to God for a life that was so captivating, so full of unfamiliar things, so challenging.

They crossed all the republics that formed a country called Yugoslavia (where two more young men—a painter and a musician—got on) without many problems. As they drove through Belgrade, the capital of Yugoslavia, Paulo thought back with affection—but without any regrets—to his old girlfriend, who had taken him on his first trip out of the country. She had taught him how to drive, to speak English, to make love. He gave in to his imagination, and he pictured her, together with her sister, running through those streets and seeking shelter during the bombings of the Second World War.

"As soon as the sirens sounded, we'd run to the basement. My mother would lay us both down across her lap, tell us to open our mouths, and cover us with her own body."

"Open your mouths? Why?"

"To keep the thunderous sound of the bombs from destroying our eardrums and leaving us deaf for the rest of our lives."

In Bulgaria, they were continually followed by a car carrying four menacing types—as part of a mutual understanding between the authorities and the bus driver. After a burst of collective joy back at the Austrian border town, the trip was getting a bit monotonous. The plan was to stop for a week in Istanbul, but they still had a ways to go before getting there—in exact figures, a hundred and twenty miles, which was absolutely nothing considering they'd already traveled almost two thousand.

Two hours later, they could see the minarets of two grand mosques.

Istanbul! They'd made it!

Paulo had worked out a detailed plan of how to spend his time here. He'd once watched the dervishes perform with their skirts twirling around them. He'd been fascinated and decided that he was going to learn how to dance like that until he finally understood it wasn't merely a dance but a way of speaking with God. They called themselves Sufis, and everything he'd read about them left him even more excited. He'd had plans to go to Turkey one day to train with the dervishes or the Sufis, but he'd always thought this was something he'd do in the distant future.

But now he was actually here! The towers getting closer, the road filled with an ever-increasing number of cars, traffic jams—more patience, more waiting—however, before the sun rose again, he would be among them.

"Set your watches: we'll be there in an hour," the driver said. "We're going to spend a week here, not because this is some touristic stop, as you've probably already guessed, but before we left Amsterdam—"

Amsterdam! It seemed like centuries ago!

"—we received a warning that, earlier in the month, an assassination attempt on the King of Jordan transformed part of our route into a minefield. I tried to get a sense of how things are developing, and it looks as if the situation has calmed down a bit, but we decided before leaving Amsterdam that we wouldn't risk it.

"We'll continue our plan a little further on—also because both Rahul and I are tired of the same thing over and over and we need to eat, drink, have a little fun. The city is cheap, in fact, it's *dirt cheap,* the Turks are incredible, and the country, despite everything you'll see on the streets, is not Muslim but secular. All the same, I'd advise our beauties to avoid wearing more provocative clothing and our beloved young men that they not provoke any fights just because someone's made some sort of joke about their long hair."

He'd given them fair warning.

"One more thing: back in Belgrade, when I called in to say that everything was all right, I learned that someone called looking to do an interview about what it means to be a hippie. The agency said it was important because it would get word out about its services—and I didn't have the presence of mind to argue.

"The journalist in question knew where we were going to stop to fill up our tank and our stomachs, and was waiting for me there. He peppered me with questions, but I wasn't sure how to respond to any of them—all I said was that your bodies and souls are free like the wind. This journalist—he's from a major French news agency—wanted to know if he could send somebody from his Istanbul bureau to speak directly with one of you, and I told him I didn't know but that we would all be staying in the same hotel—the cheapest we could manage to find, each room with space for four . . ."

"I'll pay extra, but I'm not sharing a room. My daughter and I will take a room for two."

"Same here," said Rayan. "Room for two."

Paulo gave Karla a searching look, and she finally responded. "Room for two here, too."

The bus's other muse liked to show she had the skinny Brazilian under her thumb. They'd spent much less money than they'd imagined up until then—mostly because they lived off sandwiches and slept on the bus more times than not. Days earlier, Paulo had counted his fortune—eight hundred and twenty-one dollars, after endless weeks of traveling. The monotony of recent days had softened Karla's mood a bit, and their bodies were already coming into more frequent contact—they'd sleep resting their heads on one another's shoulders, and now and then they held hands. It was an extremely comfortable, caring feeling, though they'd never ventured more than a kiss—no other form of intimacy.

"Anyway, there ought to be a journalist waiting. If any of you don't want to talk, you're not required to say anything. I'm only telling you what I was told."

The traffic began to move faster.

"I forgot to say something very important," said the driver, after whispering an exchange with Rahul. "It's easy to find drugs on the street—from hashish to heroin. As easy as in Amsterdam, Paris, Madrid, or Stuttgart, for example. Except that, if they catch you, no one—absolutely no one—will manage to get you out of the slammer in time to leave with us. You've been warned. I hope I've made myself very, very clear."

They'd been warned, but Michael had his doubts that anyone would heed this warning, especially because they'd spent almost three weeks without touching any sort of drug. Though he kept careful watch on every one of his passengers without their knowing it, during the three weeks they'd been together, he hadn't noticed anyone show interest in the things they consumed every day in Amsterdam and other European cities.

Which, once again, gave him doubts: Why was it everyone loved to say drugs were addictive? As a doctor, someone who, while in Africa, had experimented with several hallucinogenic plants to see if he could use them on his patients, he knew that only those derived from opium caused any dependency.

Ah yes, and cocaine, which rarely made its way to Europe since the United States consumed nearly everything that was produced in the Andes.

Still, governments everywhere spent fortunes on antidrug campaigns while cigarettes and alcohol were sold in every corner bar. Perhaps that explained why everyone loved to say drugs were addictive: political agendas, advertising budgets, that sort of thing.

He knew that the Dutch girl who'd just asked for a room

with the Brazilian had doused one of the pages of her book in an LSD solution—she'd mentioned it to others. Everyone knew everything on the bus, an "Invisible Post" was in effect. When the time was right, she would cut a piece, chew it, swallow, and wait for the resulting hallucinations.

But that wasn't a problem. Lysergic acid, discovered in Switzerland by Albert Hofmann and popularized throughout the world by Timothy Leary, a Harvard professor, had been declared illegal but remained indetectable.

Paulo awoke with Karla's arm across his chest—she was still in a deep sleep—and lay there thinking about how to adjust his position without waking her.

They'd arrived at the hotel relatively early, the entire group had eaten dinner at the same restaurant—the driver was right, Turkey was dirt cheap—and when they went up to their rooms he found a double bed in his. Without saying anything, he and Karla took a shower, washed their clothes, hung them in the bathroom to dry, and—exhausted—collapsed on the bed. By the look of it, the two of them were thinking only about sleeping in a decent bed for the first time in days, but their naked bodies, touching for the first time, had different plans. Before they knew it, they were kissing.

Paulo had trouble getting an erection, and Karla didn't help; she made it clear that she was interested only if he was. It was the first time they'd gone beyond kissing and handholding; just because he had a beautiful woman at his side, was he required to pleasure her? Would she feel less beautiful, less desired if he didn't?

And Karla thought: let him suffer a bit, thinking I'll be upset if he decides to sleep instead. If I see things aren't progressing as I'd like, I'll do what I have to do, but let's wait and see.

An erection finally came, and then penetration, and Paulo reached orgasm quicker than either of them thought possible, no matter how much he'd tried to hold back. After all, it had been a long time since he'd had a woman at his side.

Karla, who hadn't reached any sort of orgasm, and Paulo knew it, gave him an affectionate tap on the head, like a mother to her child, turned to the other side of the bed, and realized right at that moment just how exhausted she was. She slept without thinking about any of the things that usually helped her to fall asleep. Paulo did the same.

Now that he was awake, he thought back to the previous night and decided to step out before he was forced to have a conversation about it. He carefully removed her arm, put on an extra pair of pants that was in his backpack, threw on some shoes and his jacket, and just as he was about to open the door, he heard:

"Where are you going? Aren't you at least going to say good morning?"

"Good morning." *Istanbul must be a pretty interesting place and I'm sure you're going to like it.*

"Why didn't you wake me up?"

Because I think sleeping is a way of talking to God through our dreams. That's what I learned when I began to study the occult.

"Because you could have been having a beautiful dream or maybe because you must be exhausted. I don't know."

Words. More words. Words only served to complicate matters.

"Do you remember last night?"

We made love. Without thinking about it much, for no other reason than we were both naked in the same bed.

"I remember. And I wanted to say sorry. I know it wasn't what you were expecting."

"I wasn't expecting anything. Are you going to meet Rayan?"

He knew she was really asking, "Are you going to meet Rayan and *Mirthe*?"

"No."

"Do you know where you're going?"

"I know what I'm looking for. I just don't know where it is—I need to ask at reception, I hope they can tell me."

He hoped her questioning would end there, that she wouldn't force him to tell her what he was looking for: somewhere he could find the dancing dervishes. But she did ask him.

"I'm going to a religious ceremony. Something to do with dancing."

"You're going to spend your first day in such a different city, such a special country, doing exactly what you already did in Amsterdam? Weren't the Hare Krishna enough? Or the night around the bonfire?"

It had been enough. And, with a mixture of annoyance and a desire to provoke her, he told her about the dancing Turkish dervishes that he'd seen in Brazil. The men wearing tiny red caps on their heads, immaculately white skirts, begin by slowly turning around themselves—as though they were Earth or some other planet. That movement, after a certain time, ends up driving the dervishes into a sort of trance. They're part of a special order, at turns recognized and abominated by Islam, the order's principal source of inspiration. The dervishes belonged to an order called Sufism, founded by a thirteenth-century poet who was born in Persia and died in Turkey.

Sufism recognizes a single truth: nothing is divisible, the visible and the invisible are one, each of us is merely an illusion in flesh and bone. That was why he had little interest in the bus conversation about parallel realities. We are everyone and everything at the same time—time that, by the way, does not exist. We forget this because we are bombarded daily with information from the newspaper, the radio, the TV. If we accept the Unity of Existence, we have need of nothing else. We will understand the meaning of life for a brief moment, but this brief moment will grant us the strength to make it until what they call death, which in reality is our passage into circular time.

"Understand?"

"Perfectly. For my part, I'm going to the bazaar—I imagine Istanbul must have a bazaar—where there are people working day and night to show the few tourists who make it here the purest expression of their souls: art. Of course, I don't plan on buying anything—and it's not a question of frugality, but lack of space in my backpack—but I'll make an effort, a real effort, to see if people understand me, understand my admiration and respect for what they're doing. Because for me, despite the whole philosophical speech you've just given me, the only language that matters is called Beauty."

She walked to the window, and he watched her naked silhouette against the sun outside. No matter how annoying she tried to be, he felt a deep respect for her. He left wondering whether it wouldn't be better to go to a bazaar—it would be difficult to access the reclusive world of the Sufis, no matter how much he'd read about them.

And Karla stood in the window thinking: Why hadn't he invited her to go with him? After all, they had six more days there, the bazaar wasn't about to close, and coming into contact with a tradition like Sufism must be an unforgettable experience.

They were, yet again, traveling in opposite directions, no matter how hard they tried to reach one another.

Karla found most of the bus group downstairs, and everyone invited her to join them on a special excursion—to the Blue Mosque, the Hagia Sophia, and the archaeological museums. There was no lack of unique tourist attractions—for example, a gigantic cistern, with twelve rows of columns (a total of 336, someone commented) that in the past had served to store the water supply destined for Byzantine emperors. But she told them she had other plans, and no one asked any questions—just as no one asked any questions about her having spent the night in the same room as the Brazilian. They all ate breakfast together and each group set off for its destinations.

Karla's destination, in theory, wasn't in any guidebook. She walked to the edge of the Bosphorus and stood staring at the red bridge dividing Europe from Asia. A bridge! Connecting two such different, distant continents! She smoked two, three cigarettes, lowered the straps a bit on the nondescript top she was wearing, getting a little sun until three or four men came up and tried to start a conversation—and soon she was forced to pull her top back over her shoulders and move on.

Ever since boredom had set in among everyone on the trip, Karla had begun to face herself and her favorite question: *Why do I want to go to Nepal? I was never one to believe much in these things; my Lutheran upbringing is stronger than any incense, mantras, sitting postures, meditation, sacred books, or esoteric sects.* She didn't want to go to Nepal to find answers to these things—she already had them, and she was tired of the need to make a constant show of her strength, her courage, an unwaning aggressivity, her uncontrollable competitiveness. All she'd ever done in her life was outrun others, but she would never be able to outrun herself. She had gotten used to who she was, despite her young age.

She wanted everything to change, but was incapable of changing herself.

She would have liked to say many more things to the Brazilian than she had, make him believe that with each passing day she was becoming an ever more important part of his life. She felt a morbid pleasure in knowing that Paulo had left feeling guilty for the awful sexual experience of the night before and the fact that she had done nothing to reassure him with sweet words: "Don't worry, my love [my love!], the first time is always like that, we're just getting to know each other."

But circumstances didn't allow her to get any closer to him, or anyone else. Either because she lacked patience with others, or because others weren't much help, weren't trying to accept her as she was—the first thing they did was keep their distance, incapable of a bit of effort to break through the icy wall she was always hiding behind.

She was still capable of love, without expecting anything—changes, gratitude—in return.

And she had loved many times in her life. Whenever this had happened, love's energy transformed the universe around her. Whenever this energy appears, it always manages to do its work—but things were different with her, she couldn't stand to love for very long.

She yearned to be a vase where Love would come and leave its flowers and its fruit. Where the living water would preserve them as though they'd just been picked, ready to be delivered to whoever had the courage—yes, "courage" was the word—to seize them. But no one like that ever showed up—or, more accurately, people would no sooner show up than they would flee in fear because she was no vase but a storm of lightning, wind, and thunder, a force of nature that could never be tamed or merely channeled to stir windmills, light up cities, sow terror.

She wished they could see her for her beauty, but all anyone ever saw was the hurricane, and they never sought shelter from it. They preferred to flee to safer ground.

Her thoughts turned again to her family—though they were practicing Lutherans, they'd never sought to impose their beliefs. Once or twice, when she was a child, she'd been spanked, which was normal and hardly traumatic—everyone who lived in her city had been through the same thing.

She had excelled in school, was terrific at sports, was the most beautiful of all her classmates (and knew it), and had never had any trouble finding a boyfriend. Even so, she preferred her solitude.

Solitude. Her greatest pleasure. The origin of her dream of traveling to Nepal was to find a cave and remain there alone until her teeth fell out, her hair became white, the local villagers stopped bringing her food; spending her final sunset looking at the snow, nothing more.

Alone.

Her school friends envied her easygoing way with the boys, her college friends admired her for her independence and for knowing exactly what she wanted, and the people at work were always stunned and surprised by her creativity—in the end, she was the perfect woman, queen of the mountain, the lioness of the jungle, savior of lost souls. She had received marriage proposals since the day she turned eighteen, from all sorts of people—but above all, rich men, who added to their proposals a series of collateral benefits, such as gifts of jewelry (two diamond rings—of the many she'd received—were enough to pay for her ticket to Nepal and leave plenty to live on for a long time to come).

Anytime she received an expensive gift, she warned her suitor that she would not return it in the event they separated. The men would chuckle; they were used to being challenged by other men, more powerful than she, and didn't take her seriously. They ended up falling into the abyss she'd created around herself, and it was then they realized that in reality they'd never gotten close to the fascinating girl, but stood on a fragile bridge made of wire unable to support the weight of the same things day after day. Another week, a month, and the inevitable moment of separation would arrive, and it was never necessary to say a thing—none of them had the courage to ask for anything back.

Until, three days into their relationship, as they ate breakfast in their fancy hotel room in Paris, where they'd gone for a book launch (no one refused a trip to Paris, it was one of her mottoes), one of these suitors told her something she would never forget:

"You're depressed."

She laughed. They barely knew each other, they'd just had dinner at an excellent restaurant, drunk the best wine and the finest champagne, and that was what he had to tell her?

"Don't laugh. You suffer from depression. Or anxiety. Or both. But the fact of the matter is that, as you get older, you'll find yourself at the point of no return. The earlier you accept this the better."

She felt like telling him just how much luck she'd had in her life; she had a wonderful family, a job she liked, the admiration of others—but something else came out.

"Why would you say a thing like that?"

Her voice was full of scorn. The man, whose name she made a point of forgetting that same afternoon, didn't want to talk about it—psychiatry was his profession, and he wasn't there to work.

She insisted. Perhaps, deep down, he wanted to talk about it—at this point, she had the impression he was dreaming about spending the rest of his life at her side.

"We've been together so little time, what makes you say I'm depressed?"

"Because this little time amounts to forty-eight hours at your side. I've had the chance to observe you during the book launch

Tuesday, and yesterday at dinner. Have you, by chance, ever loved anyone?"

"Many people."

It was a lie.

"What does it mean to love?"

The question frightened her so much she came up with everything she could think of to answer it. Casting her fear aside, she responded in a measured voice.

"It's to allow everything. To not spend your time thinking about the sunrise or enchanted forests, to not swim against the current, to allow yourself to be filled with joy. That, for me, is what it means to love."

"Go on."

"It's to maintain your freedom, but in such a way that the person at your side never feels trapped by this. It's a calm, serene thing, I'd even say it's solitary in some way. Love for love's sake, for no other reason—such as marriage, children, money, that sort of thing."

"Fine words. But as long as we're together, I suggest you think about what I've told you. Let's not ruin our stay in such a special city by my making you question yourself and your making me work."

OK, you're right. But why tell me I suffer from depression or anxiety? Why so little interest in the things I have to say?

"Why would I be depressed?"

"One possible answer is that you've never truly loved. But at this point such an answer isn't good enough—I know plenty of depressed people who come to me because they've loved too much, so to speak—they've given themselves up entirely. To be

188

honest, I think—I shouldn't be saying this—that your depression has some physical origin. A lack of a certain substance in your body. Could be serotonin, dopamine, but in your case it certainly isn't noradrenaline."

So depression was a chemical problem?

"Of course not. There are a million factors, but do you think we could get dressed and go walk along the Seine?"

"Of course. But before we do, finish your thought: What factors?"

"You said that one can love in solitude; there's no doubt about that, but only those who've dedicated their lives to God or their neighbors. Saints. Visionaries. Revolutionaries. In this case, I'm talking about a more human love, which can only be felt when we're near the person we love. A love that makes us suffer terribly when we can't express it, or when we're noticed by the object of our affections. I'm certain you're depressed because you're never truly present; your eyes shift from one side to the other, there's no light behind them, just weariness. On the night of the book launch, I saw you were making a superhuman effort to speak with the others there—everyone must seem dull, inferior, all the same."

He got up from the bed.

"That's enough for me. I'm going to take a shower, or do you want to go first?"

"Go ahead. I'm going to pack my suitcase. Don't rush, I need a few minutes alone after everything I just heard. Actually, I need a half hour alone."

He chuckled, as if to say, "What did I tell you?" But he went into the bathroom. Five minutes later, Karla had packed her suitcase and put on her clothes. She opened and closed the door without making any noise. She walked past the reception desk, greeting all those people looking at her with a certain air of surprise, but the luxurious suite wasn't in her name, so no one asked her anything.

She went up to the concierge and asked what time the next flight to Holland left. Which city? Doesn't matter, I'm from there and know my way around. Two-fifteen in the afternoon, KLM. "Would you like us to buy the ticket and charge it to the room?"

She paused for a second; maybe she ought to get back at the man who'd read her soul without permission and who, besides, could have been wrong about everything.

But she didn't. "No, thanks, I have the money here." Karla never traveled anywhere depending on the men who every now and then decided to keep her company.

She took another look at the red bridge and remembered everything she'd read about depression—and everything she hadn't read because she'd begun to really get scared—and she decided that, from the moment she crossed that bridge, she would be a new woman. She'd allow herself to fall for the wrong person, some guy who lived on the other side of the world, to miss him when he was gone or do everything to remain at his side, or sit meditating and recalling his face in whatever cave in Nepal she chose to live in, but she couldn't continue living that life—the life of someone who has it all and can't ever enjoy any of it.

Paulo stood before a door without a sign or any other indicator on it, in the middle of a narrow street lined with houses that looked abandoned. After considerable effort and many questions, he'd manage to locate a Sufi center, though he wasn't sure he'd find any dancing dervishes. He'd managed to get there by going to the bazaar—where he'd waited for Karla but never found her; then he began to mimic the sacred dance while repeating the word "dervish." Several people laughed, others thought he was crazy—they all kept their distance to avoid being hit by his outstretched arms.

He kept his composure; in several stores he saw the same hat he'd seen the dervishes wearing—some kind of red, cone-shaped beanie, generally associated with the Turks. He bought one, placed it on his head, and continued walking through aisle after aisle, mimicking the dance—this time with the hat—and asking where he could find a place where people did such things. This time, no one laughed or scurried past, they merely gave him a serious look and said something in Turkish. But Paulo wasn't about to give up.

He finally found a white-haired old man who seemed to understand what he was saying. He'd continued to repeat the word "dervish" and was beginning to grow tired. He had six more days here, maybe he'd take advantage of the fact that he was there and see the bazaar, but the old man drew closer and said:

"*Darwesh.*"

Ah, that must have been it, he'd been pronouncing it wrong the entire time. As though to confirm his suspicion, the man began imitating the dance of the dervishes. The man's expression changed from surprise to condemnation.

"You Muslim?"

Paulo shook his head.

"No," the man said in English. "Only Islam."

Paulo stepped in front of him.

"Poet! Rumi! *Darwesh!* Sufi!" he said, also in English.

The name Rumi, as the founder of the order was called, and the word *poet* must have softened the old man's heart. Though he pretended to be annoyed and unwilling, he grabbed Paulo by the arm, dragged him out of the bazaar, and brought him to the spot where Paulo found himself at that moment, in front of a house that was nearly in ruins, unsure exactly what to do other than knock on the door.

He knocked several times, but no one answered. He turned the handle, the door was unlocked. Should he go in? Could he be accused of trespassing? Wasn't it true that abandoned buildings had wild dogs looking after them to keep out the homeless?

He opened the door a crack. He stood there waiting to hear dogs barking, but instead he heard a voice, a single voice in the distance, saying something in English that he couldn't make out, and he immediately noticed a sign that he was in the right place: the smell of incense.

He made a great effort to discover what the man's voice was saying. He couldn't make out a thing, the only way was to go inside—the worst that could happen was that they'd turn him away. What was there to lose? Suddenly, he was about to realize one of his dreams: to connect with the dancing dervishes.

He had to take the risk. He walked in, closed the door behind him, and when his eyes had adjusted to the relative darkness of the place, he saw that he was in a completely empty coach house, painted entirely in green, the wood floor worn by the years. A few broken windows allowed the light to filter in and made it possible to discern, in a corner of that space which seemed much larger inside than it had from out front, an old man sitting on a plastic chair talking to himself, which he stopped doing as soon as he noticed the unexpected visitor.

He said a few words in Turkish, but Paulo shook his head. He didn't speak Turkish. The man shook his head, too, demonstrating his displeasure at the presence of a stranger who'd interrupted something important.

"What do you want?" he asked with a French accent.

What could Paulo say? The truth. Dancing dervishes.

The man laughed.

"Perfect. You came here just as I did when I left Tarbes—a tiny little town in the middle of nowhere in France with a single mosque—in search of knowledge and wisdom. That's what you want, isn't it? Do what I did when I found one of them. Spend a thousand and one days studying a poet, memorizing everything he wrote, answering any questions anyone ever has with the wisdom of his poems, and then you can begin your training. Because your voice will have begun to mix with that of the Enlightened One and the verses he wrote eight hundred years ago."

"Rumi?"

The man bowed upon hearing the name. Paulo sat on the floor.

"And how can I learn? I've already read much of his poetry, but I don't understand how he put it into practice."

"A man in search of spirituality knows little, because he reads of it and tries to fill his intellect with what he judges wise. Trade your books for madness and wonder—then you will be a bit closer to what you seek. Books bring us opinions and studies, analyses and comparisons, while the sacred flame of madness brings us to the truth."

"I'm not carrying many books. I came as a person in search of an experience—in this case, the experience of dance."

"This is a search for knowledge, not dance. Reason is the shadow of knowledge of Allah. What power does the shadow have before the sun? Absolutely none. Come out from the shadow, go to the sun, and allow its rays to inspire you, not words of wisdom."

The man pointed to a spot where a ray of sunlight had entered, some thirty feet from his chair. Paulo walked over to the place indicated.

"Salute the sun. Allow it to fill your soul—knowledge is an illusion, ecstasy is the true reality. Knowledge fills us with guilt, ecstasy allows us to be one with He who is the Universe before it existed and after it has been destroyed. The search for knowledge is an attempt to wash oneself with sand when a well of clean water can be found right next to us."

At that exact moment, the loudspeakers mounted in the mosque towers began to recite something, the sound filled the city, and Paulo knew it was the call to prayer. His face was turned to the sun, a lone ray visible on account of the dust, and he knew from the noise behind him that the old man with the French accent must have fallen to his knees, turned his face toward Mecca and started to pray. Paulo began emptying his mind; it wasn't so difficult, not in that place bereft of any ornament—not even the words of the Koran written in that script that looked like a painting. He had reached total emptiness, far from home, his friends, the things he'd learned, the things he still wanted to learn, from good or evil, he was there. Just there, in the moment.

He bowed, and then lifted his head again, keeping his eyes open, and he saw the sun was speaking with him—it wasn't trying to teach him anything, merely permitting its light to flood everything around him.

My loved one, my light, may your soul persist in unending adoration. At some moment you will leave the place you are now and return to your own people, because the time to renounce all has not yet arrived. But the Supreme Gift, called Love, will make you an instrument of My words—the words I've not spoken but which you understand.

The silence will teach you if you give yourself up to the Great Silence. This silence may be translated into words, because this will be your destiny, but when this happens, seek no explanations, and urge others to respect the Mystery.

So you want to be a pilgrim on the pathway of the Light? Learn to roam the desert. Speak with your heart, because words are a question of mere chance—though you need them to communicate with others, do not be misled by meanings and explanations. People hear only what they want to hear, never seek to persuade anyone, only follow your destiny without fear—or even filled with fear, but follow your destiny.

Do you wish to reach Heaven and come to me? Learn to fly with two wings—discipline and mercy.

Temples, churches, and mosques are full of people afraid of what's to be found outside—and end up indoctrinated by lifeless words. My temple is the world, do not leave it. Though it may be difficult, remain in the world—even should you be the target of others' laughter.

Speak with others but do not seek to persuade them. Never allow others to believe in your words or become your disciples, for when this occurs, they no longer believe in what their hearts tell them, which in truth is the only source to which they must listen.

Walk hand in hand, drink and be merry with life, but keep your distance such that one never relies on the other—our fall is part of the journey and we all must learn to rise again on our own.

The minarets had gone silent. Paulo wasn't sure how long he'd been speaking with the sun—its single ray lit a spot far from where he was seated. He turned around, and the man who'd come from a distant country merely to find what he could have found in the mountains of his own country had already left. Paulo was alone there.

It was time to leave, he was slowly relinquishing himself to the sacred flame of madness. He would have no need to explain

196

to anyone where he'd been and hoped his eyes were still the same—he could feel them gleaming, and this could attract others' attention.

He lit a stick of incense next to the chair and left. He closed the door but knew that, for those who seek to step beyond the threshold, the door is always open. You need only turn the knob.

The woman from the French news agency was visibly upset by the assignment she'd been given: to interview hippies—hippies!—in the middle of Turkey, as they made their way to Asia by bus like the many immigrants who came in the opposite direction in search of wealth and opportunity in Europe. She had no prejudice against either group, but now that conflicts had flared in the Middle East—the telex printer never ceased vomiting up news, there were rumors of battalions killing each other in Yugoslavia, Greece was on the edge of war with the Turks, the Kurds wanted autonomy and the president wasn't sure what to do, Istanbul had become a nest of spies from the KGB and CIA, the King of Jordan had crushed a rebellion, and the Palestinians were promising revenge. What exactly was she doing in this third-class hotel?

Following orders. She'd receive the call from the driver of the so-called Magic Bus, an experienced and kind man who waited for her in the lobby of the hotel, and who also struggled to understand the interest of the foreign press in the subject but had decided to help however he could.

She scanned the lobby, there wasn't a single hippie to be found, only a man who looked like Rasputin and another man about fifty years old, with no trace of hippie about him, seated next to a young woman.

"He's the one who will answer your questions," the driver said, gesturing to the fifty-year-old, who had traveled all this way in the company of his daughter. "He speaks your language."

The advantage was they could converse in French; that would make the interview much quicker and easier. She began by placing them in time and space (Name: Jacques / Age: 47 / Birthplace: Amiens, France / Profession: Former director at a leading French cosmetics firm / Marital status: Divorced).

"As I'm sure they've told you, I'm here working on an article for Agence France-Presse about this culture that, from what I've read, has its origin with the Americans . . ."

She kept herself from saying the "rich little playboys without anything better to do."

". . . and has swept across the entire globe."

Jacques nodded, while the journalist thought once again of adding "or actually, wherever rich people live."

"What exactly do you want to know?" he asked, regretting having agreed to the interview because the rest of the group was out exploring the city and having a good time.

"So, we know that it's a movement without prejudices, based on drugs, music, huge open-air concerts where anything goes, travel, absolute and total disregard for those who are fighting at the moment for an ideal, a free, a more just society . . ."

"For example . . ."

"For example, those trying to liberate the oppressed,

200

denounce injustice, take part in the essential class struggle, in which people give their blood and their lives so that the only hope for humanity, socialism, might no longer be mere utopia and instead become a reality."

Jacques nodded—it was useless to react to that sort of provocation, the only thing he'd do would be lose his precious first day in Istanbul.

"And who have a much freer, I would say more débauché, view of sex, where middle-aged men have no problem being seen next to girls young enough to be their daughters . . ."

Jacques was about to let this one pass, too, but then another voice cut in.

"The girl young enough to be his daughter—I'm guessing you're referring to me—is, in fact, his daughter. We weren't introduced; my name is Marie. I'm twenty years old, born in Lisieux. I study political science, admire Camus and Simone de Beauvoir. Musical tastes: Dave Brubeck, the Grateful Dead, and Ravi Shankar. At the moment, I'm writing a dissertation about how the socialist paradise people are laying down their lives for, also known as the Soviet Union, has become every bit as oppressive as the dictatorships imposed on the Third World by capitalist countries like the United States, England, Belgium, France. Anything else you want to know?"

The journalist thanked her for her response, swallowed hard, considered for a second whether the girl was lying, decided she was not, then sought to hide her surprise and concluded that this, perhaps, was the guts of her article: the story of a man, a former director at a French multinational, who in a moment of existential crisis decides to abandon everything, take his daughter with him, and set off around the world—without considering the risks this could entail for the girl, or, in this case, young woman. Or precociously wise old woman, judging by her way of speaking. She found herself at a disadvantage and needed to recover her initiative.

"Have you experimented with drugs?"

"Of course: marijuana, mushrooms, a few chemical drugs that made me sick, LSD. I've never touched heroin, or cocaine, or opium."

The journalist looked over at her father, who listened calmly at his daughter's side.

"And are you one of these who supports free love?"

"Ever since they invented the pill, I see no reason why love shouldn't be free."

"And do you put this into practice?"

"That's none of your business."

The father, seeing they were headed for a confrontation, decided to change the subject.

"Aren't we here to talk about hippies? You provided an excellent summary of our philosophy. What more do you want to know?"

Our philosophy? A man on the cusp of fifty was talking about "our philosophy"?

"I want to know why you're going to Nepal by bus. From what I understand, and from what I can tell from the clothes the two of you are wearing, you have enough money to go by airplane."

"Because the most important thing to me is the journey. It's meeting people I'd never have the opportunity to meet flying first class on Air France, as I've done so often before—no one talks to anyone there, even if they're sitting next to one another for twelve hours."

"But there are . . ."

"Yes, there are buses that are more comfortable than this rickety old school bus with terrible suspension and seats that don't recline—I imagine that's what you were wanting to say. It just so happens that in my previous incarnation—in other words, during my career as a director of marketing—I'd already met everyone I needed to know. And, to tell you the truth, each of them was a copy of the others—the same rivalries, the same interests, the same ostentation, a life completely unlike that of my childhood, when I worked at my father's side in a field near Amiens."

The journalist began to leaf through her notebook; she was clearly at a disadvantage. It was difficult to provoke these two.

"What are you looking for?"

"The phrase I wrote down about the hippies."

"But you summed us up so well: sex, drugs, rock, and travel."

The Frenchman was managing to get deeper under her skin than even he imagined.

"You think that's all there is to it. But it's so much more."

"So much more? Then show us, because when I decided to come on this trip, at my daughter's invitation, I could see just how unhappy I was. I didn't have time to exactly figure out the details."

The journalist said it was all right, she had what she needed—and she thought to herself: I could make up whatever I want from this interview, no one would ever know. But Jacques wasn't about to give up. He asked her if she wanted a coffee or tea ("Coffee, I'm tired of this sweetened mint tea"), Turkish coffee or regular ("Turkish coffee, I'm here in Turkey; it really is ridiculous to filter out the liquid, the grains ought to be there, too").

"I think that my daughter and I deserve to learn a bit. We aren't sure, for example, where the word *hippie* comes from." He was clearly being ironic, but she pretended not to notice and decided to carry on. She was dying for a coffee.

"Nobody knows. But, if we were to be very French about it and try to find a definition for everything, the idea of sex, vegetarianism, free love, and communal living has its origin in Persia, in a cult founded by a guy named Mazdak. We don't know much about him. However, as we were finding ourselves forced to write more and more about this movement, a few journalists came upon a different origin: among the Greek philosophers known as the Cynics."

"Cynics?"

"Cynics. Nothing to do with the meaning we give the word today. Diogenes was the group's most famous proponent. According to him, we ought to set aside whatever society imposes on us—all of us were raised to have more than we need—and return to primitive values. In other words, be in touch with the laws of nature, depend on little, find joy in each new day, and completely reject all that we grew up with—power, gain, avarice, that sort of thing. The only purpose in life was to free themselves of what they did not need and find joy in each minute, in each breath. Diogenes, by the way, lived in a barrel, according to legend."

The driver drew closer. The hippie who looked like Rasputin

must have spoken French, because he sat on the floor to listen. The coffee arrived. This gave the journalist the energy to continue her lesson. Suddenly the general air of hostility had disappeared, and she was the center of attention.

"The idea spread during Christianity, when monks would walk into the desert in search of the necessary peace to speak with God. And it is with us until today, through well-known philosophers like the American Thoreau or the liberator of India—Gandhi. Keep it simple, they all say. Keep it simple and you shall be happy."

"But how did this suddenly become a sort of trend, a way of dressing, of being a cynic in the current meaning of the word—not believing in Left or Right, for example?"

"That I couldn't tell you. Some say it happened with the giant rock concerts, like Woodstock. Others say it was certain musicians, like Jerry Garcia and the Grateful Dead, or Frank Zappa and the Mothers of Invention, who began to give free shows in San Francisco. That's why I'm here asking the two of you."

She looked at her watch and rose to her feet.

"I'm sorry, I have to go. I have two more interviews today."

She grabbed her papers, adjusted her clothes.

"I'll show you to the door," Jacques said. Any hostility had disappeared entirely—she was simply someone looking to do her job well and not an enemy who had come there to bad-mouth those she was interviewing.

"No need. There's also no need to feel bad for what your daughter said."

"I'll accompany you all the same."

They left together. Jacques asked her where he could find

the spice bazaar—he had no interest in seeing things he wasn't about to buy, but he was dying to breathe in the aroma of plants and herbs whose scents he might never have another chance to experience.

The journalist pointed the way and set off, her footsteps quick, in the opposite direction.

As he walked to the spice bazaar, Jacques—who had worked for so many years selling things that no one needed, forced to create a new campaign every six months to excite consumers about the "new product" that had just been launched—thought to himself that Istanbul ought to have a more effective tourism department: he was absolutely fascinated by its narrow streets, the tiny shops he passed, the cafés frozen in time—their decor, people's clothes, the mustaches. Why did the vast majority of Turkish men grow a mustache?

He found the answer entirely by chance after stopping off in a bar that must have seen better days, its decoration entirely art nouveau, the kind you find only in the most hidden and sophisticated spots in Paris. He decided then to have his second Turkish coffee of the day—grains and water, no filter, served in a sort of copper cup with a stem on the side instead of a handle, something that he'd only seen there. He hoped that by the end of the day the stimulating effects would have left his body and he would be able to get another night of rest. The place wasn't very full—actually, there was only one other client—and the owner, seeing that he was a foreigner, struck up a conversation.

The owner asked about France, England, Spain; he told the story of his Café de la Paix, he wanted to know what Jacques thought of Istanbul ("I just got here, but it seems to me more people ought to know about it"), the great mosques and the Grand Bazaar ("I still haven't seen any of that, I got here yesterday"), and then he began to talk about the excellent coffee he served, until Jacques interrupted him.

"I noticed something interesting, and I might be wrong. But, at least in this part of the city, everyone has a mustache—including you, sir. Is this some tradition? You don't have to answer if you don't want."

The bar owner seemed thrilled to answer.

"I'm so glad you noticed—I think that's the first time a foreigner has come in here and asked me this. And listen, on account of my excellent coffee, the few tourists who do visit come here quite often, on the recommendation of the nicer hotels."

Without asking permission, the owner sat down at Jacques's table and asked his helper—a kid who'd barely made it past puberty, his face beardless—to bring him a mint tea.

Coffee and mint tea. That was all people seemed to drink in this country.

"Religious, then?"

"Me?"

"No, the mustache."

"Not at all! It has to do with the fact that we're men—with honor and dignity. I learned this from my father, who had a very finely manicured mustache, and who always said to me,

'One day you'll have one just like this.' He taught me that, during my great-grandfather's generation, when the damn English and—forgive me—French began to drive us to the sea, people had to decide on a direction forward. And, as each battalion was a nest of spies, they decided that a mustache would act as a sort of code. Depending on the way it was trimmed, it meant a person was either in favor of or against the reforms that the damn English—and, forgive me again, French—were seeking to impose. It wasn't exactly a secret code, of course, but a declaration of principles.

"We've been doing this since the end of the glorious Ottoman Empire, when people were forced to determine a new path for the country. Those who were in favor of the reform wore a mustache in the shape of an M. Those who were against it allowed the sides of the mustache to grow downward, forming a sort of upside down U."

And those who were neither for nor against?

"They shaved their entire faces. But it was shameful for those men's families—as though they were women."

"And that's still true today?"

"The father of all the Turks—Kemal Atatürk, the army officer who finally managed to bring to an end the era of thieves put on the throne by the European powers, sometimes wore a mustache and sometimes not. This confused everyone. But once traditions are established, it's difficult to forget them. Not to mention, coming back to the beginning of our conversation, what harm does it do for a person to demonstrate his masculinity? Animals do the same thing with their fur or feathers."

Atatürk. The courageous army officer who'd fought in the

First World War, staved off an invasion, abolished the sultanate, put an end to the Ottoman Empire, separated Islam from the state (which many had judged impossible). And, what was more important to the damn English and French, he refused to sign a humiliating peace treaty with the Allies—as Germany had done. A treaty that unintentionally planted the seeds of Nazism.

Jacques had already seen several photos of the greatest icon of modern Turkey—when the company where he'd worked had tried to conquer that empire once again, employing seduction and malice. He had never noticed that at times Atatürk appeared without a mustache; he'd noticed only that in the photos where he had a mustache he wore it in neither the shape of an M nor the shape of a U but in the Western tradition, in which the whiskers come to the ends of the lips.

My goodness, he'd learned so much about mustaches and their secret messages! He asked how much he owed for the coffee, but the bar owner refused payment: he'd charge him the next time.

"Many Arab sheikhs come here for mustache implants," the man concluded. "We're the best in the world."

Jacques traded a few more words with the owner, who soon excused himself because his lunch clients were beginning to arrive. Jacques handed money to the beardless kid for the coffee and left, silently thanking his daughter for having literally pushed him to leave his job, with an excellent severance package. What if he were to return from his "vacation" and tell his work friends about mustaches and the Turks? They'd all find it interesting, exotic, but nothing more.

He kept walking toward the spice bazaar and thinking to himself: *Why didn't I ever, ever force my parents to leave the fields of Amiens for a bit and go travel?* In the beginning, the excuse was that they needed money so their only son could receive a proper education. When he earned his degree in marketing— something his parents didn't even understand—they said perhaps they would travel abroad for their next vacation, or the one after that, or perhaps the one after that, though every farmworker knows that nature's work is never finished and that farming alternates between moments of backbreaking work— planting, pruning, harvesting—and moments of extreme boredom, spent waiting for nature to complete its cycle.

The truth is they never had any intention of leaving the region they knew so well, as though the rest of the world were a dangerous place where they would end up lost along unfamiliar streets, in strange cities full of snobby people who would immediately notice their country accents. No, the whole world was the same. Each person had his place and that ought to be respected.

Jacques had often become exasperated as a child and adolescent, but there was nothing to do except carry on his life just as he'd planned: find a good job (he did), find a woman to marry (he was twenty-four when this happened), build a career, travel the world (he did and ended up exhausted from living in airports, hotels, and restaurants while his wife patiently waited at home, in search of a meaning for her life beyond her daughter). At some point he would be promoted to director, retire, go back to the country, and spend the rest of his days in the place he was born.

Looking back all these years later, he thought he could have skipped those intermediary stages—but his spirit and his enormous curiosity had propelled him forward, toward endless hours of work at a job he loved at the beginning and began to hate just as he was moving up the ladder.

He could have waited a little and left at the right moment. He was quickly advancing through the ranks, his salary had tripled, and his daughter—whom he'd watched grow in stages between one trip and another—had begun to study political science. His wife ended up divorcing him because she felt her life had no purpose, and now she lived alone because Marie had found a boyfriend and moved to his house.

Most of his ideas about marketing (a word and a profession then in vogue) were accepted, though some were questioned by attention-seeking interns. He was used to this and soon clipped the wings of anyone trying to "prove himself." His end-of-year bonuses, based on company profits, grew and grew. Now that he was single again, he had started partying more and found himself girlfriends who were both interesting and out for their own interests—his cosmetics firm was known to everyone, his girlfriends were always dropping hints that they would like to appear in promotional ads for certain products, and he neither refused nor promised. Time passed, the self-interested girlfriends left, and the sincere ones wanted him to marry them, but he already had his future planned: ten more years of work and he would get out at the height of middle age, full of money and possibilities. He would travel the world, this time to Asia, which he didn't know too well. He would try to learn things that his daughter, by this point also his best friend, would like to teach him. They dreamed of going to the Ganges and to the Himalayas, the Andes and Ushuaia, near the South Pole—after he'd retired, of course. And, obviously, after she graduated.

Until two events shook up his life.

The first occurred on May 3, 1968. He was waiting for his daughter at the office so they could take the metro home; after more than an hour, she still hadn't arrived. He decided to leave a note at the reception desk in the building where he worked, near Saint-Sulpice (the company had several buildings and his department did not occupy offices in the company's luxurious headquarters), and left, ready to continue on to the metro alone.

Suddenly, without warning, he saw that Paris was burning. Black smoke filled the air, sirens were everywhere, and the first thing he thought of was the Russians—they'd bombed the city!

But soon he was pushed against a wall by a group of kids running through the street, their faces covered with damp cloths, shouting "Down with the dictatorship!" and other things he no longer remembered. Behind them, heavily armed police launched tear-gas canisters. Some of the kids had tripped and fallen, and those left behind were immediately beaten by the police.

His eyes began to burn on account of the gas. He couldn't

understand what was happening—what was the meaning of all this? He needed to ask someone, but most important at that moment, he needed to find his daughter—where could she be? He tried walking toward the Sorbonne, but the streets were completely blocked, by pitched battles between the forces "of order" and what looked to be a bunch of anarchists from some horror film. Tires burned, rocks were being thrown at the police, Molotov cocktails flew every which way, public transportation had ground to a halt. More tear gas, more shouting, more sirens, more rocks being torn from the pavement, more kids being beaten—where is my daughter?

Where is my daughter?

It would be a mistake—not to mention suicide—to walk toward the conflict. It was best to walk toward home, wait to hear from Marie, and allow everything to pass. It all ought to be over that night.

He had never taken part in student protests, he had other aims in life, but no protest that he had seen had ever lasted more than a few hours. All that was left was to wait for his daughter to call—that was all he asked God for at that moment. They lived in a country with so many privileges, where young people had everything they wanted. The adults knew that if they worked hard they could retire without any worries, continue drinking the world's best wine, eating the world's best food, and walking through the most beautiful city in the world without the worry of being mugged.

His daughter's phone call came around two in the morning—he'd kept the television on; the two public TV channels were

216

showing and analyzing, analyzing and showing, what was going on in Paris.

"Don't worry, Daddy. I'm all right. I should pass the telephone to the person next to me, so I'll explain later."

He tried to ask her something, but she'd already hung up.

He couldn't sleep at all the entire night. The protests had lasted much longer than he had imagined they would. The talking heads on TV were as surprised as he was. Everything had exploded from one moment to the next, without warning. But they tried to demonstrate calm and make sense of the confrontations between police and students using the pompous explanations of sociologists, politicians, analysts, a few policemen, a few students, and the like.

Finally, the adrenaline had left his blood and he'd collapsed, exhausted, on the couch. When he opened his eyes it was already morning, time to go to work, but someone on the television—it had been on the entire night—was warning people not to leave the house; the "anarchists" had occupied the universities and metro stations, closing streets and blocking traffic. Violating the fundamental rights of every citizen, someone added.

He called in to work; no one answered. He called the headquarters, and someone who had spent the night there because he lived in the suburbs and had no way to get home told him it was useless to try to move around the city. Almost no one, only those who lived close to the office, had managed to make it in.

"It will all be over today," said the anonymous voice on the other end of the line. Jacques asked to talk to his boss, but like many others, his boss hadn't gone to work either.

The chaos and the conflicts hadn't ceased as expected. On the contrary, the situation worsened when people saw the way the police were treating the students.

The Sorbonne, symbol of French culture, had been occupied, and professors there had joined the protests or been expelled from the premises. Several committees had been formed with aims that would be either carried out or abandoned, the TV said, by this point showing more sympathy for the students.

The stores in his neighborhood were closed, except for one run by an Indian man—and there was a line of people out the door. He patiently joined the line, listening to the others around him: "Why doesn't the government do anything?" "Why do we pay such high taxes only to find the police so inept at a moment like this?" "This is all the fault of the Communist Party." "This is all happening because of the way we raised our kids, they think they have the right to turn against everything we taught them."

That sort of thing. The only thing no one was able to explain was why it all was happening.

The first day passed.

Then the second.

The first week came to an end.

And everything got worse and worse.

His apartment was situated on a tiny hill in Montmartre, three subway stations from his office. From his window, he could hear the sirens and see the smoke rising from burning tires. He stared endlessly at the street as he waited for his daughter to arrive. She showed up three days later, took a quick shower, grabbed some of her clothes—since they were at his apartment—ate whatever she could find, and left again, repeating, "I'll explain later."

What he'd thought would be a fleeting moment, a contained fury, ended up spreading over all of France; employees kidnapped their bosses, and a general strike was declared. Most factories were occupied by workers—just as had happened a week earlier with the universities.

France came to a standstill. The problem was no longer the students—who seemed to have changed their focus and now waved flags emblazoned with FREE LOVE or DOWN WITH CAPITALISM, or OPEN BORDERS FOR ALL, or THE BOURGEOISIE DON'T UNDERSTAND A THING.

The problem now was the general strike.

The TV was his only source of information. That was where he saw, to his surprise and horror, after twenty hellish days, the president of France finally appear to tell his countrymen that he would organize a referendum proposing "cultural, social, and economic renewal." If he lost, he would resign. General Charles de Gaulle, he who had survived the Nazis, he who had put an end to the colonial war in Algeria, he who was admired by all.

What de Gaulle had to propose meant nothing to the workers, who had little interest in free love, open borders, that sort of thing. They thought of only one thing: a meaningful increase in wages. Prime Minister Georges Pompidou met with union leaders, Trotskyites, anarchists, socialists, and only then did the crisis begin to wane—when everyone was face-to-face, each group making different demands. This division was the government's doing.

Jacques decided to take part in a pro–de Gaulle demonstration. All of France watched in horror. The demonstration, which spread to nearly every city, brought together an enormous number of people, and those who had launched what Jacques never stopped calling "anarchy" soon recoiled. New labor agreements were signed. The students, who no longer had any demands, slowly returned to classes—overcome with the sensation that their victory meant absolutely nothing.

At the end of May (or beginning of June, he couldn't remember), his daughter finally came back home and told him they had achieved everything they wanted. He didn't ask her what it was they wanted, and she didn't elaborate, but she looked tired, disappointed, frustrated. Restaurants were opening once again. They had a candlelight dinner and avoided the subject entirely. Jacques wasn't about to tell her he'd gone to a rally in support of the government. The only comment he took seriously, very seriously, was when she said:

"I'm tired of this place. I'm going to travel and live far away from here."

In the end, she gave up on the idea; first she needed to "finish her studies," and Jacques understood that those who desired a prosperous, competitive France had won. True revolutionaries weren't the least bit worried about graduating and earning a diploma.

Ever since that day, he'd read thousands of pages full of explanations and justifications offered by philosophers, politicians, editors, journalists, et cetera. They cited the closing of a university in Nanterre earlier that month, but that couldn't have been the reason for the fury he'd witnessed the few times he had dared to leave the house.

He never saw a single line that could bring him to conclude: "Ah, that's what started it all."

The second—and defining—transformative moment was a dinner in one of Paris's finest restaurants, where he would bring special clients—potential buyers for their countries and cities. France had already turned the page on May 1968, though its flames had spread to other locations across the globe. No one wanted to revisit these events and if a foreign client dared to ask about them, Jacques would discreetly change the subject, arguing that "the newspapers always exaggerate."

And the conversation would end there.

He was a good friend of the restaurant's owner; they were on a first-name basis, which impressed his clients—part of the plan, by the way. He would walk in, the waiters would take him to "his table" (which was always changing according to how busy it was, but his guests didn't know this). A glass of champagne was immediately served to each of the guests, the menus delivered, the orders taken, the expensive wine ("Same as always, right?" the waiter would ask, and Jacques would nod), and the conversation was always the same (leaving those who had just arrived wondering if they ought to go to the Lido, the Crazy Horse, or the Moulin-Rouge; it was incredible how Paris was reduced to these three destinations in foreigners' minds). There was no talk of work during a business dinner unless it came at the end, when an excellent Cuban cigar was offered to everyone at the table. The final details were worked out among people who thought they were extremely important when in reality the sales department had everything ready and only needed the proper signatures, as was always the case.

After everyone had ordered, the waiter turned to Jacques: "The usual?"

The usual: oysters for an appetizer. He explained how they must be served alive; seeing how the majority of his guests were foreigners, they were horrified. His plan was to order snails next—the famous escargots. He'd end by asking for a plate of frog legs.

No one dared join him, and that was how he preferred it. It was part of the marketing.

All the appetizers were served at the same time. The oysters arrived, and everyone else sat waiting to see what would happen next. He squeezed a bit of lemon over the first, which moved a bit, to the surprise and horror of his guests. He popped it in his mouth and allowed it to slide down into his stomach, savoring the salt water that always remained in the shell.

Then, two seconds later, he could no longer breathe. He tried to maintain his pose, but it was impossible—he dropped to the floor, certain he was about to die, looking at the ceiling and its crystal chandeliers, possibly brought from Czechoslovakia.

His vision began to change; now he could see only black and red. He tried to sit—he'd already eaten dozens, hundreds of oysters in his life—but he no longer had any control over his own body. He tried to pull air into his lungs, but it refused to enter.

There was a quick moment of anxiety, and then Jacques died.

Suddenly, he was hovering near the restaurant ceiling looking down on a crowd that had gathered around his body. Others tried to make room for help to arrive, as the Moroccan waiter ran toward the kitchen. His vision wasn't exactly sharp and clear; it was as though there was a transparent veil or some sort of water running between him and the scene below. Fear, and everything else, had ceased to exist—an immense peace washed over everything, and time, because time still existed, sped up. The people down below seemed to move in slow motion, in other words, in photograms. The Moroccan waiter returned from the kitchen, and the images disappeared—the only thing left was complete, white emptiness, and a peacefulness that was almost palpable. Contrary to what many said on occasions like that, he saw no dark tunnel; he felt a loving energy all around him, something he hadn't experienced in a long time. He was a baby in his mother's womb, nothing more—he never wanted to leave there again.

Suddenly he felt a hand grabbing him and pulling him down. He didn't want to go; he was finally enjoying what he'd fought and waited for his entire life—peace, love, music, love, peace. But the hand was tugging him with incredible force and he was unable to fight against it.

The first thing he saw when he opened his eyes was the restaurant owner's face, somewhere between worried and overjoyed. His heart was racing, he felt nauseous, like he was about to vomit, but he controlled himself. He'd broken out in a cold sweat, and one of the waiters brought a tablecloth to cover him.

"Where was it you found this lovely pale tone and beautiful blue lipstick?" the owner asked him.

His guests, sitting around him on the floor, also appeared relieved and terrified. He tried standing up, but the owner stopped him.

"Rest. This isn't the first time this has happened here and it won't be the last, I imagine. That's why we, along with most restaurants, are required to have a first-aid kit, with bandages, disinfectant, a defibrillator in case of heart attack, and, luckily, the adrenaline injection we've just given you. Do you have the phone number of some relative? We're calling an ambulance, but you're entirely out of danger. They're going to ask the same thing, but if there's no one, I imagine one of your companions here can go with you."

"The oyster?" were his first words.

"Of course not—our products are of the highest quality. But we don't know what they eat—and, by the looks of things, this little friend of ours, rather than create a pearl, took advantage of your illness and decided to try to kill you."

What was it then?

At that moment, the ambulance pulled up. The paramedics tried placing him on a stretcher, but he said he was all right. He needed to believe this and got up with a bit of effort, but the paramedics laid him out again, this time on the stretcher. He decided not to argue or say anything at all. They asked for a phone number for next of kin. He gave his daughter's, and that was a good sign; he was able to think clearly.

The paramedics took his blood pressure, ordered him to follow a certain light with his eyes, to put his finger on the tip of his nose. Every order obeyed, he was itching to get out of there. He didn't need any hospital, even if he did pay a fortune in taxes to have a health service that was excellent and free.

"It's likely we're going to keep you overnight for observation," they told him as they walked toward the ambulance at the door, where people peered in from the street, always happy to see someone in worse shape than they were. There was no limit to human morbidity.

On their way to the hospital, the siren turned off (a good sign), he asked whether it had been the oyster. The paramedic at his side confirmed what the owner had told him. No. Had it been the oyster, it would have taken longer, even hours.

So what was it?

"An allergy."

He asked them to explain in more detail—the restaurant owner had said that it must have been something the oyster ate, and, again, they confirmed this. No one knew how or when such a reaction would occur—but they knew how to treat it. The technical name for it was "anaphylactic shock." Without trying to frighten him, one of the paramedics told him that allergies can appear without any warning. "For example, you might have eaten pomegranates since you were a kid, but one day one might kill you in minutes for reasons we can't explain. For example, a person spends years caring for his garden, the herbs are the same, the pollen hasn't changed, until one day he begins coughing, feels a pain in his throat, then in his neck, thinks he's catching cold and ought to go inside, but suddenly he can no longer walk. But it isn't a sore throat, it's the trachea closing up. *Troppo-tardi*. And this happens with things we've come in contact with our entire lives.

"Insects may be more dangerous, but even so we're not going to spend our entire lives afraid of bees, am I right?

"Don't be afraid. Most allergies aren't serious and don't select their victims by age. What's serious is anaphylactic shock, like you had—the rest mean a runny nose, red bumps on the skin, itching, that sort of thing."

They made it to the hospital, where his daughter was waiting. She already knew her father had suffered an acute allergic reaction, that it could have been fatal had help not arrived in time, but that such cases were incredibly rare. They went to a private room—Marie had already given the hospital their insurance number, so it wasn't necessary to go into one of the common rooms.

He changed clothes—in her haste, Marie had forgotten to bring his pajamas, so he wore a gown provided by the hospital. The doctor came in, took his pulse—it was back to normal; his blood pressure was still a little high, but he blamed this on the stress he'd felt in the last twenty minutes. The doctor asked Marie not to stay too long, told her the next day her father would be home.

She pulled a chair up next to the bed, took her father's hands, and suddenly Jacques began to cry. At first, they were only silent tears, but they soon transformed into hiccups, which increased in intensity, and he knew that he had needed that release, so much so that he made no effort to control himself. The tears flowed, and his daughter simply patted his hands affectionately, half-relieved, half-scared. It was the first time she'd seen her father cry.

He wasn't sure how long the moment lasted. He slowly became calmer and calmer, as though a weight had been taken from his shoulders, his chest, his head, his life. Marie thought it was time to let him sleep and began to remove her hand, but he held it there.

"Don't leave. I need to tell you something."

She laid her head on her father's lap, like she'd done when she was a child listening to his stories. He ran his fingers through her hair.

"You know that you're fine and can go back to work tomorrow, don't you?"

Yes. He knew. And the next day he would go to work—not to the building where he had his office but to the headquarters. The current director had come up through the company together with Jacques and had sent a message saying he'd like to see him.

"I want to tell you something: I was dead for a few seconds, or minutes, or an eternity—I don't have a sense of the time because things happened so slowly. And suddenly I saw myself surrounded by a loving energy I'd never felt before. It was as though I were in the presence . . ."

His voice began to tremble, like that of someone holding back tears. But he continued.

". . . as though I were in the presence of God. Something that, as you know, I've never believed in. I only decided to send you to Catholic school because it was close to our house, and the education, excellent. I was required to participate in religious ceremonies, which bored me to death, filled your mother with pride, and made your classmates and their parents see me as one of them. But the truth is it was merely a sacrifice I made for your sake."

He continued stroking his daughter's head—it had never occurred to him to ask whether she believed in God or not, because the moment wasn't right. As far as he could tell, she no longer followed the strict form of Catholicism she'd been raised in; she was always wearing exotic clothing and hanging out with friends with long hair, listening to music much different from Dalida or Edith Piaf.

"I always had everything planned out, I knew how to carry out these plans, and according to my time line, soon I'd be retired with enough money to do what I like. But all this changed in those minutes or seconds or years when God took me by the hand. As soon as I returned to the restaurant floor and the worried expression of the owner feigning calm, I understood that I could never go back to living the way I had before."

"But you like your job."

"I liked it so much I was the best at what I did. But now I want to say goodbye to this work that's filled with warm memories. Tomorrow, I want to ask you a favor."

"Anything. You've always been a father who taught me more by your example than by the things you told me."

"That's exactly what I want to ask you. I taught you many things for years and now I want you to teach me. I want us to travel the world together, to see things I've never seen, to pay closer attention to the morning and the night. Quit your job and come with me. I hope your boyfriend can indulge me a bit, patiently await your return, and allow you to come with me.

"I need to immerse my soul and my body in rivers I've not yet known, drink things I've not yet drunk, contemplate mountaintops I've only seen on television, allow the same love that I felt tonight to return, even if it's only for a minute each year. I want you to lead me through your world. I will never be a burden, and when you feel I ought to go off on my own, you need only ask and I'll do it. And when you feel the time is right to return, I'll do that and we'll take one more step together. I'll say it again: I want you to lead me."

His daughter didn't move. Her father hadn't merely returned to the world of the living but had found a door or window that opened onto his own world—which she would never dare share with him.

The two of them thirsted for the Everlasting. Quenching this thirst was simple—they needed only to allow the Everlasting to appear to them. To do so, they needed no special place beyond their own bodies and faith, a shapeless force that runs through everything and carries within it what the alchemists call anima mundi.

Jacques reached the front of the bazaar, where more women were entering than men, more children than adults, fewer mustaches and more head scarves. From where he stood he could detect a strong scent—a mixture of perfumes that combined into one and climbed toward the heavens before returning again to Earth, bringing with the rain a blessing and a rainbow.

Karla's tone had softened when they met in the hotel room to change into the clothes they'd washed the day before, as they prepared to head out to dinner.

"Where did you end up going today?"

She had never asked him this—to his mind, this was something that his mother would ask his father, or other married adults their partners. He didn't feel like answering, and she didn't insist.

"I'll bet you went to the bazaar looking for me," she said, and began to laugh.

"I started walking in your direction, but soon I changed my mind and went back to the place I was before."

"I have an offer that you can't refuse: let's have dinner in Asia."

It didn't take much effort to figure out what she was proposing: to cross the bridge that led from one continent to the next. But the Magic Bus would be doing this soon, why the hurry?

"Because one day I'll be able to tell people something they'll never believe. I had a coffee in Europe and twenty minutes later

I walked into a restaurant in Asia, ready to eat all the delicious things to be found there."

It was a good idea. He would be able to tell his friends the same thing. No one would believe him either; they'd think the drugs had gone to his brain, but what did he care? There really was a drug that had slowly begun to take effect, it had started that afternoon, with the very same man he'd found when he entered the empty cultural center with its walls painted green.

Karla must have bought some sort of makeup at the bazaar, because she left the bathroom with eye shadow, and mascara on her lashes, something he'd never seen. She wore a constant smile, something he'd also never noticed before. Paulo thought about shaving—he'd had a goatee for ages, which covered his prominent chin, but generally he shaved whenever possible, and being unable to do so brought back horrifying memories, such as the days he'd spent in prison. But it hadn't occurred to him to buy one of those disposable razors—he'd thrown away the last one just before they crossed into Yugoslavia. He put on a sweater he'd bought in Bolivia and the jean jacket with the metallic stars, and they walked downstairs together.

There was no one from the bus in the hotel lobby, except the driver, entertaining himself with the newspaper. They asked how they could cross the bridge to Asia. The driver smiled.

"I can tell you. I did the same thing my first time here."

He gave them the necessary information to grab a bus ("Don't even think about going on foot") and apologized for forgetting the name of the excellent restaurant where he'd had lunch one time, on the opposite side of the Bosphorus.

In reality, they weren't headed for Asia but for the former Constantinople. Others had joked with the driver about this, and now he did the same thing with the young couple. Favorable delusions were always welcome.

"What's going on in the world?" Karla asked, pointing to the newspaper. The driver also seemed surprised by her makeup and her smile. Something had changed.

"Things have cooled down in the last week. For the Palestinians, who—according to the newspaper—are a majority in the country and were planning a coup, this will be forever known as Black September. That's what they're calling it. But travel routes are flowing normally—though I did call the office again and they've suggested I wait here for instructions."

"Great, no one's in any hurry. There's an entire world to discover here in Istanbul."

"You two need to visit Anatolia."

"All in good time."

As they walked toward the bus stop, Paulo noted that Karla held his hand as though they were something they were not—boyfriend and girlfriend. They made small talk, there was a lovely full moon that night, it wasn't windy or rainy, it was perfect dining weather.

"I'll pay today," she said. "I'm dying to drink something."

They boarded the bus and crossed the Bosphorus in reverential silence—as though having a religious experience. They got off at the first stop and walked along the edge of Asia, where there were five or six restaurants with plastic tablecloths. Seating themselves at the first one they came to, they looked out at the view before them; Istanbul's monuments weren't lit as in Europe, but the moon took it upon itself to cast over the city the most beautiful light they'd ever seen.

A waiter approached to take their order. They asked him to choose the best and most traditional dish. The waiter wasn't used to this.

"But I need to know what you want. Here, everyone typically knows what they want."

"We want the best. Isn't that a good enough answer?"

No doubt it was. And the waiter, rather than complaining again, accepted the fact that the foreign couple was placing their trust in him. Which was an incredible responsibility, but at the same time, an incredible joy. "And what would you like to drink?"

"The best local wine. Nothing European; we're in Asia, after all."

They were dining in Asia, together, for the first time in their lives! "Unfortunately we don't serve alcoholic beverages here. Strict religious regulations."

"Turkey is a secular country, is it not?"

"Yes, but the owner is religious." If they wanted to change restaurants, they could find what they were looking for two blocks away. Two blocks away they would have their wine but lose the magnificent view of Istanbul bathed in moonlight. Karla asked herself if she could manage to say everything she wanted to say without drinking. Paulo didn't hesitate—this would be a dinner without wine.

The waiter brought a red candle inside a metal lantern, lit it in the center of the table, and while all this happened, neither of them said a thing. They imbibed the surrounding beauty and were soon drunk with it.

"We were telling each other about the days we had. You said you started off toward the bazaar to find me but soon changed your mind. A good thing, because I wasn't at the bazaar. We'll go tomorrow, together."

She was behaving quite differently, remarkably mellow—which wasn't typical of her. Had she found someone and needed to share her experience?

"You begin. You left there saying you were going after a religious ceremony. Did you find one?"

"Not exactly what I was looking for, but I found something."

I knew you would return," said the man without a name when he saw the young man in colorful clothes walk through the door. "I think you must have had a powerful experience because this place is filled with the energy of the dancing dervishes. Although, I must stress: every place on Earth contains the presence of God in the tiniest things—insects, a grain of sand, everything."

"I want to learn the ways of the Sufi. I need a teacher."

"Then seek the Truth. Seek always to be on its side, even when it brings you pain. There are times when the Truth goes quiet for long stretches, or when it doesn't tell you what you want to hear. That's Sufism. The rest is a series of sacred rites that do nothing more than intensify this state of ecstasy. But in order to take part in them, it's necessary to convert to Islam, something I truly cannot recommend. There's no need to join a religion on account of its rituals alone."

"But I need someone to lead me along the path toward truth."

"That's not Sufism. Thousands of books have been written about the path toward Truth, and none of them explain what it is exactly. Humanity has committed its greatest crimes in the name of the Truth. Men and women were burned alive, entire civilizations were destroyed, those who committed sins of the flesh were sent away, those who pursued a different path were cast out. One of them, in the name of 'truth,' was crucified. But before dying, he clarified Truth's ultimate definition. It is not that which gives us certainty. It is not that which gives us profound thoughts. It is not that which makes us better than others. It is not that which makes us prisoners to our own prejudices. 'The Truth is what makes us free. You will know the Truth and the Truth shall set you free,' Jesus said."

He paused.

"Sufism is nothing more than bringing yourself up-to-date, shifting your mind, understanding that words lack the power to describe the Absolute, the Infinite."

The food arrived. Karla knew exactly what Paulo was saying, and everything she would tell him when her turn came would be based on his words.

"Let's eat in silence?" she asked. Once again, Paulo found her behavior unusual—normally she would have pronounced those words with an exclamation point at the end.

Yes, they ate in silence. Gazing at the sky, the full moon, the waters of the Bosphorus glowing beneath its rays, their faces illuminated by candlelight, their hearts bursting at the meeting of two strangers who suddenly enter another dimension together. The more we allow the world in, the more we receive—be it love, be it hate.

But at that moment it was neither one nor the other. Paulo wasn't seeking any revelations, he didn't respect any tradition, he'd forgotten what was dictated by sacred texts, logic, philosophy, everything.

He had entered a state of complete emptiness, and this emptiness, through its inherent contradiction, filled everything.

They didn't ask what they'd been served—they only knew that there were tiny portions spread across many plates. They didn't have the courage to drink the water, so they ordered soda—safer, though certainly much less interesting.

Paulo ventured the question that was burning him up, the question that could have ruined the night, but he couldn't control himself any longer.

"You're completely different. Have you found someone and fallen in love? You don't need to answer, if you don't want to."

"I have found someone and I am in love, though he doesn't know it."

"Is that what happened today? Is that what you wanted to tell me?"

"Yes. When you're done with your story. Or did you already finish?"

"No, but I need to tell it through to the end, because the story has yet to find its ending."

"I'd like to hear the rest."

There was no anger in her response to his question, and he tried concentrating on the food—no man likes to hear these things, especially from the woman with whom he's dining. He always wants her to be entirely there, focused on the moment, on the candlelight dinner, the moonlight falling over the water and the city.

He began to try each dish—pasta stuffed with meat in the shape of ravioli, rice rolled up in tiny cigars made from grape leaves, yogurt, unleavened bread fresh from the oven, beans, skewers of meat, several sorts of pizza in the shape of boats and stuffed with olives and spices. Their dinner would last an eternity. But, to their surprise, the food soon disappeared from the table—it was too delicious to leave there to grow cold and lose its flavor.

The waiter returned, cleared the plastic plates, and asked whether he could bring the main dish.

"No way! We're much too full!"

"But we're already making it, we can't stop now."

"We'll happily pay for it, but *please* don't bring anything else or we won't be able to walk afterward."

The waiter laughed. They laughed. A strange wind blew in, bringing unexpected things with it, filling everything around them with unfamiliar flavors and colors.

It had nothing to do with the food, the moon, the Bosphorus, or the bridge—but with the day both of them had had.

"Will you tell me the rest?" Karla asked, lighting two cigarettes and handing him one. "I'm dying to tell you about my day and how I found myself."

By the look of it, she'd found her soul mate. In reality, Paulo no longer had any interest in his own story, but she'd asked him to tell her, and now he'd tell it to the end.

His mind returned to the green room with the paint peeling from the rafters and the broken windows that once must have been true works of art. The sun had already gone down, the room was filled with darkness, and it was time to go back to his hotel, but Paulo began to question the man without a name.

"But you, sir, must have had a teacher."

"I had three—none of them related to Islam or familiar with the poetry of Rumi. As I learned, my heart asked the Lord: Am I on the right path? He responded: You are. But I insisted: Who is the Lord? He responded: You are."

"Who were your three teachers?"

The man smiled, lit the blue hookah at his side, released a few puffs, offered it to Paulo, who did the same thing, and sat on the floor.

"The first was a thief. One time I was lost in the desert and only managed to make it home late into the night. I'd left my key with the neighbor, but I didn't have the courage to wake him at that hour. Finally, I found a man, asked for help, and he opened the lock in the blink of an eye.

"I was quite impressed and begged him to teach me how to do it. He told me he'd spent his life robbing other people, but I was so grateful I invited him to sleep in my house.

"He spent a month in my home. Every night he would go out, saying: 'I'm going to work; continue your meditation and make sure to pray.' When he returned, I always asked whether he'd managed anything. Invariably, he responded: 'Nothing tonight. But, God willing, I'll try again tomorrow.'

"He was a happy man, and I never saw him looking desperate due to a lack of results. During a good part of my life, I didn't succeed in talking to God, I meditated and meditated and nothing happened. I remembered the thief's words—'Nothing tonight. But, God willing, I'll try again tomorrow.' This gave me the strength to carry on."

"And who was the second person?"

"A dog. I was walking to the river for a drink when the dog appeared. He, too, was thirsty. But as he neared the river, he saw another dog there—it was nothing more than his reflection.

"He was frightened, turned back, barked, did everything he could to free himself of the other dog. Nothing happened, of course. Finally, because his thirst was immense, he decided to face the situation and flew headlong into the river; at that moment, the image disappeared."

The man without a name paused before continuing.

"Finally, my third teacher was a child. He was walking to the mosque near the village where he lived, with a burning candle in his hand. I asked him: 'Was it you who lit this candle?' He told me that it was. As I was worried by children playing with fire, I asked again: 'Boy, at one moment this candle was not lit. Can you tell me where the flame that now burns came from?'

"The boy laughed, put out the candle, and asked me in return: 'And you, sir, can you tell me where the flame has disappeared to?'

"At that moment, I understood how stupid I had always been. Who ignites the flame of wisdom? Where does it disappear to? I understood that, just like that candle, at certain moments man carries the sacred flame in his heart but never knows where it comes from. From that moment on, I began to pay closer attention to everything around me—clouds, trees, rivers, and forests, men and women. And everything gave me the knowledge I needed at the moment I needed it. I've had thousands of teachers throughout my life.

"I began to believe that the flame would always light the way when I most needed it; I've been a disciple of life and I continue to be. I was able to learn from the simplest and most unexpected things, such as the stories parents tell their children.

"That is why nearly all of the wisdom of Sufism is not to be found in sacred texts, but in stories, prayers, dance, and contemplation."

Paulo could hear the voices once again coming from the loudspeakers of the mosques, the muezzins calling the faithful for the final prayer of the day. The man without a name kneeled facing Mecca and began to pray. When he finished, Paulo asked if he could return the next day.

"Of course," the man said. "But you won't learn anything more than what your heart wishes to teach you. All I have for you are stories and a place where you can always come when you're in search of silence—as long as we're not performing one of our religious dances."

Paulo turned to Karla.

"Your turn."

Yes, she knew. She paid the bill, and they walked to the edge of the strait. They could hear the cars blowing their horns on the bridge, but they were incapable of ruining the moon, the water, the view of Istanbul.

"Today I sat on the other side and spent hours watching the river flow. I thought back on how I've lived up until now, the men I've met, and my behavior, which never seemed to change. I was tired of myself.

"I asked myself: Why am I like this? Am I the only one, or are there others incapable of love? I've known many men in my life who were eager to do everything for me, and I never loved any of them. At times, I thought I'd finally met my Prince Charming, but this feeling didn't last long—and soon I couldn't stand the person anymore, no matter how caring, attentive, and loving he was. I didn't give any explanation, I simply told them the truth—they would try everything to win me over again, but it was useless. The simple touch of their hands on my arm, in an attempt to make things all right, repulsed me.

"I've been with people who threatened to commit suicide—thank God it was only a threat. I've never felt jealousy. At a certain time in my life, when I passed the barrier of twenty, I thought I was sick. I've never been faithful—I always found other lovers, even when I was with someone willing to do everything for me. I met a psychiatrist, or a psychoanalyst, I'm not exactly sure which, and we went to Paris. It was the first time someone noticed this, and then he started in with his labels—I needed medical attention, my body lacked some hormones. Instead of looking for help, what I did was return to Amsterdam.

"As you've no doubt noticed and imagined, I seduce men rather easily. But soon thereafter, I lose interest. That's why I had the idea of going to Nepal: I considered never returning, growing old discovering my love for God—which, I admit, until now is only something that I think I feel, but I'm not entirely sure.

"The fact is I never found an answer to my question, I didn't want to consult doctors, I simply wanted to disappear from the world and dedicate my life to contemplation. Nothing more.

"Because a life without love isn't worth living. What is a life without love? It's a tree that bears no fruit. It's sleeping without dreaming. At times, it's even an inability to sleep. It's living one day after another waiting for the sun to shine into a room that is completely shut up, painted black, where you know where the key is but have no desire to open the door and go out."

Her voice began to crack, as though she were about to cry. Paulo drew near and tried to embrace her, but she pushed him away.

"I'm still not finished. I've always been an expert at manipulating others, and this gave me such confidence in myself, in my superiority, that subconsciously I repeated to myself: I'll only give completely of myself the day someone appears who is capable of taming me. And to this day, that person has yet to appear."

She turned to him, her eyes, which one might have expected to be full of tears, were filled with sparks.

"Why are you here, in this land of dreams? Because *I wanted*. Because I needed company and I thought you were the ideal companion, even after seeing all your shortcomings—pretending you were a free man as you followed the Hare Krishna through the streets, going to that house of the rising sun to show how brave you were, when really it was just stupid. Accepting my invitation to see a windmill—*a windmill!*—as if you were taking a trip to Mars."

"You insisted."

Karla hadn't insisted, she'd merely made a suggestion, but apparently her suggestions were generally taken as orders. She continued, without bothering to explain further.

"And that was the day, when we came back from seeing the windmill and went after what *I* wanted—to buy the ticket to Nepal—that I realized I was falling for you. Not for any particular reason, nothing had changed from the day before, it wasn't any gesture or thing that you'd said—absolutely nothing. But I was falling hard. And I knew, as I had each time before, that this feeling wouldn't last long—you're completely wrong for me.

"I kept waiting for the feeling to pass, but it never did. When we started talking to Rayan and Mirthe, I felt jealous for the first time. I'd been envious, angry, insecure before, but jealous?

Jealous wasn't part of my universe. I thought you all should have been paying more attention to me, this independent, beautiful, intelligent, strong-willed woman. I decided it wasn't exactly jealousy of Mirthe that I felt but envy at the fact that I wasn't the center of attention at that moment."

Karla took his hand.

"And then this morning, as I sat watching the river and remembered the night we danced together around the bonfire, I discovered it wasn't some temporary infatuation I felt—no, nothing like that, it was love. Even after our intimate moment last night, when you showed just how bad a lover you could be, I was still in love with you. When I sat on the bank of the strait, I was still in love with you. I know that I love you and I know that you love me. And that we could spend the rest of our lives together, on the road, in Nepal, in Rio, on a desert island. I love you and I need you in my life.

"Don't ask me why I'm telling you this now—I've never said this to anyone, and you know I'm telling you the truth. I love you and I'm not looking to explain my feelings."

She turned to face him, waiting for Paulo to kiss her. There was something strange in his kiss, and he said maybe it was better they return to Europe, to the hotel—it had been a full day, full of emotions and absolute fascination.

Karla felt afraid.

Paulo was even more afraid; the truth was he was having a beautiful adventure with her—there were moments of passion, moments he never wanted her to leave his side, but all that was over.

No, he didn't love her.

250

In the morning, people met for breakfast to trade experiences and recommendations. Karla tended to sit alone—when asked about Paulo, she said that he wanted to take advantage of every second to understand more about the so-called dancing dervishes, and so he would meet someone every morning who could teach him more.

" 'The monuments, the mosques, the cisterns, the marvels of Istanbul can wait,' he told me. 'They'll always be there. But I'm learning about something that could disappear from one moment to the next.' "

The others understood perfectly. After all, as far as they could tell, the relationship between the two went no further than having split a room.

The night they returned from Asia, just after dinner, they made amazing love that left her soaked in sweat, satisfied, and ready to do anything for this man. But he was talking less and less.

She didn't dare ask him the obvious question—Do you love

me?—she was simply sure of it. Now she wanted to set her own needs aside and let him go meet this Frenchman he'd been talking about and learn as much as he could about Sufism; after all, it was a unique opportunity. The young man who looked like Rasputin invited her along to the Topkapi Palace Museum, but she declined. Rayan and Mirthe asked her to go with them to the bazaar—they'd been so caught up with everything else that they'd forgotten the most important thing: How did people live there? What did they eat? What did they buy? She said yes, and they agreed to meet the following day.

The driver told her it was either that day or never—the fighting in Jordan was under control, and they ought to leave the next day. He asked Karla to tell Paulo, as though she were his girlfriend, his lover, his wife.

She responded, "Of course," whereas at other moments she would have said something like what Cain said of Abel: "Am I my brother's keeper?"

Upon hearing the driver's word, people began to voice their displeasure. But how? Weren't they going to stay an entire week in Istanbul? It was only the third day, and the first day didn't even count—they'd been too tired to do anything.

"No. We were going—and we're still going—to Nepal. We stopped here because we had no other option. And now we have to leave quickly because the conflict could rear its head again, according to the newspapers and the company I work for. Besides, there are people in Kathmandu waiting to make the return trip."

The driver had the last word. Whoever wasn't ready to leave

at eleven the following morning would have to wait for the next bus—fifteen days later.

Karla decided to go to the bazaar with Rayan and Mirthe. Jacques and Marie joined them. They noted something different in her, a lightness, a glow, though no one dared say a thing. This girl, who'd always been sure of herself and her decisions, must have fallen for the skinny Brazilian with his goatee.

Meanwhile, she thought to herself: Hmmm, the others must have noticed that I'm feeling different. They don't know the reason, but they've noticed.

What a wonderful thing it was, being able to love. She understood now why it was so important to so many people—actually, for everyone. She remembered, with a certain sorrow in her heart, how much suffering she must have sown—but there was nothing to be done, that's love.

It's what makes us understand our mission on Earth, our purpose in life. Whoever lives with this in mind will be followed by a shadow of goodness and protection, will find peace in difficult moments, will give everything without demanding anything in return, only the presence of the lover, the holder of light, the vessel of fertility, the torch that shines the way.

That's how things ought to be—and the world would always be kinder to those who love; evil would be transformed into good, lies into truth, violence into peace.

Love defeats those who would oppress it with its sensitivity, quenches the thirst of those in search of the living water of affection, keeps an open door so that the light and blessed rain can enter.

It makes the time pass more slowly or quickly, but time never passes as before—at the same monotonous, unbearably monotonous pace.

The changes within her were slow because true change requires time. But something was changing.

Before they went out, Marie came up to Karla.

"You said something to the Irish couple about some LSD you brought, didn't you?"

She did. It was impossible to detect, because she'd soaked one of the pages of *The Lord of the Rings* in an LSD solution. She'd set it out to dry back in the Netherlands, and now it was merely a passage in one of the chapters of Tolkien's book.

"I'd really like—really like—to try some today. I'm fascinated by this city, I need to see it with new eyes. Could it help me do that?"

Yes, it could. But for someone who'd never taken it, it could be heaven or it could be hell.

"My plan is simple. We go to the bazaar, then I get 'lost' there and take it far away from everybody so as not to bother anyone."

She had no idea what she was talking about. Experience your first trip alone, without bothering anyone?

At first, Karla deeply regretted having told anyone she'd brought a "page" of acid. She could have told the girl she'd heard wrong, she could have said she was referring to the characters in the book, but she hadn't mentioned any book at all. She could have said she didn't want the karma from introducing someone, especially Marie, to any sort of drug. Even more so at a moment in which her life had changed forever, because once you love someone, don't you begin to love everyone?

She looked at the girl, a little younger than she was, who had the curiosity of those true warriors, the Amazons, ready to face the unknown, the dangerous, the different—not unlike what she was herself facing. She was scared, but it was good; it was good and terrifying at the same time to discover you were alive, to know that in the end something called death awaits, and still be capable of living each moment without worrying about this.

"Let's go to my room. But first I want you to promise me something."

"Anything."

"You must never leave my side. There are several kinds of LSD, and this is the most potent—you could have an amazing experience or an awful one."

Marie laughed. The Dutch girl had no idea who Marie was, the things she'd already experienced in life.

"Promise me," Karla insisted.

"I promise."

The rest of their group was ready to leave, and "girl problems" were the perfect excuse for that moment. They would be back in ten minutes.

Karla opened the door and felt proud to show off her room; Marie saw the clothes hung out to dry, the window open to let in fresh air, and a bed with two pillows that looked as if a hurricane had blown through—which was in fact what had happened, taking several things with it and leaving others behind.

She walked over to her backpack, grabbed the book, opened it to page 155, and, with tiny scissors she always carried with her, cut a quarter of a square inch of paper.

Next, she handed it to Marie and asked her to chew it.

"That's all?"

"To tell the truth, I'd thought about giving you only half. But then I thought it might not have any effect, so I'm giving you the amount I used to take."

That wasn't the truth. She was giving the girl a half dose and, depending on Marie's behavior and tolerance for the drug, she'd make sure she had the real experience—she was simply waiting a bit.

"Remember what I'm telling you: it's what I used to take, it's been more than a year since I've put LSD in my mouth and I'm not sure I'll ever do it again. There are other, better ways to achieve the same effect, though I don't have the patience to try them out."

"Such as?" Marie had put the paper in her mouth, it was too late now to change her mind.

"Meditation. Yoga. Overwhelming passion. That sort of thing. Anything that makes us think about the world as though we're seeing it for the first time."

"How long until I feel the effects?"

"I don't know. It depends on the person."

Karla closed the book again and put it back in her bag. They went downstairs, and everyone walked together to the Grand Bazaar.

Back at the hotel, Mirthe had grabbed a brochure about the bazaar, founded in 1455 by a sultan who'd managed to wrest Constantinople from the hands of the pope. In an era when the Ottoman Empire ruled the world, the bazaar was the place people brought their wares, and it grew and grew to such an extent that the ceiling structures had to be expanded several times.

Even after having read this, the group was far from ready for what they would find—thousands of people walking through packed corridors, fountains, restaurants, prayer spots, coffee, rugs—everything, absolutely everything you could find in France's best department store: finely wrought gold jewelry, clothes in all styles and colors, shoes, rugs of all kinds, working artisans indifferent to those around them.

One of the merchants wanted to know if they were interested in antiques—the fact that they were tourists was written on their foreheads; it was clear from the way they looked around them.

"How many stores are there?" Jacques asked the merchant.

"Three thousand. Two mosques. Several fountains, an enormous number of places where you can have the best Turkish food. But I have some religious statuary you won't find anywhere else."

Jacques thanked him, said he'd be back soon—the merchant knew it was a lie and briefly redoubled his efforts but soon saw it was useless and wished them all a good day.

"Did you know Mark Twain was here?" asked Mirthe, who at this point was covered in sweat and somewhat frightened by what she was seeing. What if there was a fire, how would they get out? Where was the door, the tiny little door they'd used to come in? How would they keep the group together when everyone wanted to see something different?

"And what did Mark Twain have to say?"

"He said it was impossible to describe what he saw, but that it had been a much more powerful, more important experience than his visit to the city. He spoke of the colors, the immense variety of visual tones, the rugs, people conversing, the apparent chaos that nonetheless seemed to follow an order he was unable to explain. 'If I want to buy shoes,' he wrote, 'I don't need to go from store to store along the street, comparing prices and models, but simply find the aisle of shoemakers, lined up one after another, without there being any sort of competition or annoyance between them; it all depends on who is the better salesman.'"

Mirthe didn't care to mention that the bazaar had already been through four fires and an earthquake—it wasn't known how many had died because the hotel brochure said only this and glossed over any talk of body counts.

Karla noticed that Marie's eyes were glued to the ceiling, its curved beams and its arches, and she'd begun to smile as if she could say nothing beyond "incredible, absolutely incredible."

They walked at about a mile per hour. When one person stopped, the rest did, too. Karla needed some privacy.

"At this rate, we won't even make it to the corner of the next aisle. Why don't we split up and meet back at the hotel? Unfortunately—I repeat, unfortunately—we'll be leaving this place tomorrow, so we have to make the most of this last day."

The idea was greeted with enthusiasm, and Jacques turned to his daughter to take her with him, but Karla stopped him.

"I can't stay here on my own. Let the two of us discover this universe of wonders together."

Jacques noticed that his daughter didn't so much as glance at him, she merely repeated "incredible!" as she stared at the ceiling. Had someone offered her hashish when they entered the bazaar? Had she accepted? She was old enough to take care of herself—he left her with Karla, that girl who was always ahead of her time and always trying to show how much smarter and more sophisticated she was than all the rest, though she'd toned it down a bit—only a bit—during the last two days in Istanbul.

He went his way and disappeared amid the multitude. Karla grabbed Marie by the arm.

"Let's get out of here right now."

"But everything is so beautiful. Look at the colors: absolutely incredible!"

Karla wasn't asking, she was giving orders, and began to gently tug Marie toward the exit.

The exit?

Where was the exit? "Incredible!" Marie was growing increasingly intoxicated with what she saw, and completely inert, while Karla asked several people the best way out and received several different answers. She started to get nervous; that itself was as disorienting as an LSD trip, and she wasn't sure where the combination of the two would leave Marie.

Her more aggressive, more dominating manner returned; she walked first in one direction then another, but she could not find the door through which they'd entered. It didn't matter if they returned the way they'd come, but each second now was precious—the air had grown heavy, people were full of sweat, no one paid attention to anything except what they were buying, selling, or bargaining over.

Finally, an idea came to her. Instead of looking for the exit, she ought to walk in a straight line, in a single direction, and sooner or later she'd find the wall that separated the largest temple to consumerism she'd ever seen from the outside world. She charted a straight path, begging God (God?) that it also be the shortest. As they walked in the direction they'd chosen, she was interrupted a thousand times by people trying to sell their wares. She pushed past them without so much as an "excuse me" and without considering they could well push back.

Along the way she came upon a young boy, his mustache just coming in, who must have been entering the bazaar. He seemed to be looking for something. She decided to use all her charm, her seduction, her persuasiveness, and asked him to take her to the exit because her sister was suffering an attack of delirium.

The boy looked at her sister and saw that, in fact, she wasn't really there but off in some distant place. He tried making conversation, telling her that an uncle of his who worked nearby could help, but Karla begged him, saying she knew the symptoms, that all her sister needed now was a bit of fresh air, nothing more.

Rather against his will, and regretting that he was about to lose sight forever of these two interesting girls, he took them to one of the exits—less than sixty feet from where they'd been standing.

At the moment she stepped outside the bazaar, Marie came to the solemn decision to abandon her revolutionary dreams. She would never again say she was a Communist fighting to free oppressed workers from their bosses.

Yes, she'd started dressing like a hippie because now and then it was good to be in style. Yes, she'd understood her father had become a bit worried about this and had begun to furiously research what all of it might mean. Yes, they were going to Nepal, but not to meditate in caves or visit temples; their goal was to meet up with the Maoists who were preparing a large-scale rebellion against what they judged to be an outdated and tyrannical monarchy under the rule of a king indifferent to his people's suffering.

She'd been able to make contact through a self-exiled Maoist at her university who'd traveled to France to call attention to the few dozen guerrilla soldiers being massacred there.

None of that was important anymore. She walked with her Dutch companion along an absolutely unremarkable street and everything seemed to have a greater meaning that went beyond the peeling walls and people walking with heads lowered, barely glancing up.

"Do you think people are noticing something?"

"No, nothing, beyond the bright smile across your face. It's not a drug that was made to call others' attention."

Marie, meanwhile, had noticed something: her companion was nervous. She didn't sense this from the tone of Karla's voice—she didn't need to hear her say anything, but could attribute it to the "vibration" coming from her. She'd always hated the word "vibration," she didn't believe in such things—but at that moment she could see they were real.

"Why did we leave the temple we were in?"

Karla shot her a strange look.

"I know we weren't in any temple, it's just a figure of speech. I know my name, your name, our final destination, the city we're in—Istanbul—but everything looks so different, as though . . ."

It took her a few seconds as she searched for words.

". . . as though we'd walked through a door and left the entire known world behind, including our worries, our despairs, our doubts. Life seems simpler and at the same time richer, happier. I'm free."

Karla began to relax a bit.

"I can see colors I've never seen before, the sky looks alive, the clouds are forming shapes I can't understand *yet,* but I'm certain they're scrawling messages for me, to guide me from this point on. I'm at peace with myself and I don't view the world from the outside: I am the world. I carry with me the wisdom of those who've come before me and left their mark in my genes. I am my dreams."

They passed in front of a café, identical to the hundred others in that area. Marie continued murmuring "incredible!" and Karla asked her to stop because this time they really were about to enter a place relatively forbidden to them—only men went there.

"They know we're tourists and I hope they don't do anything, like kick us out. But, please, behave yourself."

And that's exactly what happened. They walked in and chose a corner table. Everyone looked at them in surprise, took a few minutes to realize the two girls weren't familiar with local customs, and went back to their conversations. Karla ordered a mint tea with lots of sugar—legend had it that sugar helped to diminish hallucinations.

But Marie was having wild hallucinations. She spoke about bright auras around people, claimed she could manipulate time and had in fact just spoken with the ghost of a Christian who'd died in battle there, in the exact spot where the café stood. The Christian soldier had found absolute peace in heaven, and was pleased at having been able to communicate again with someone on Earth. He was about to ask her to give a message to his mother, but when he understood that centuries had passed since his death—Marie had informed him—he gave up and thanked her, then vanished immediately.

Marie drank the tea as though for the first time in her life. She wanted to show with gestures and sighs how delicious it was, but Karla again asked her to control herself. Once more, Marie felt the "vibration" surrounding her companion, whose aura now revealed several radiant holes. Was this a bad sign? No. It looked as if the holes were old wounds that were now rapidly scarring over. She tried to calm her down—that she could do, starting a conversation in the middle of her trance.

"Do you have a thing for the Brazilian guy?"

Karla didn't answer. One of her light-filled holes seemed to shrink a bit, and Marie changed the subject.

"Who invented this stuff? And why don't they hand it out for free to everyone seeking to be one with the invisible, seeing how it's absolutely essential to changing our perception of the world?"

Karla told her that LSD had been discovered by chance, in the most unexpected place in the world: Switzerland.

"Switzerland? Where they only know about banks, watches, cows, and chocolate?"

"And laboratories," Karla added. LSD was originally discovered to cure some disease whose name she couldn't remember at the moment. Until its synthesizer—or inventor, as we'd say—decided, years later, to try a bit of the product that was already making millions for pharmaceutical companies around the world. He ingested a tiny amount and decided to ride home on his bike (the country was in the midst of a war, and even in a neutral Switzerland of chocolates, watches, and cows, gasoline was rationed), when he noticed everything looked different.

Karla noticed a change in Marie. She needed to get on with her story.

"Well then, this Swiss man—you're probably asking how I know this whole story, but the truth is there was a long article on this recently in a magazine I read at the library—noticed that he couldn't mount his bike . . . He asked one of his assistants to take him home, but then he thought perhaps it was better he go to a hospital instead; he must be having a heart attack. Then suddenly, and I'm using his words, or close to them, I can't remember them exactly: *'I began seeing colors I'd never seen, shapes I'd never noticed which wouldn't disappear even after I closed my eyes. It was like standing before a giant kaleidoscope opening and closing in circles and spirals, bursting into colorful fountains, flowing as though rivers of joy.'*

"Are you paying attention?"

"More or less. I'm not sure I'm taking it all in, there's a lot of information: Switzerland, bicycles, the war, a kaleidoscope—could you simplify a bit?"

Red flag. Karla ordered more tea.

"Try to concentrate. Look at me and listen to what I'm telling you. Concentrate. This awful feeling will be gone soon. I need to make a confession: I only gave you half the dose I used to take when I used LSD."

That seemed to relieve Marie. The waiter brought the tea Karla had ordered. She made her companion drink it, paid the bill, and they went out once again into the cold air.

"And what about the Swiss man?"

It was a good sign that Marie remembered where they'd left off. Karla asked herself if she'd be able to buy a sedative if the situation got worse—if the gates of hell replaced the gates of heaven.

"The drug you took was sold openly and freely at pharmacies in the United States for more than fifteen years, and you know that there they're strict about these things. It even made the cover of *Time* magazine for its benefits in treating psychiatric patients and alcoholism. Then it was made illegal because every now and then it had unexpected side effects."

"Such as . . ."

"We'll talk about those later. Now, try to move away from the gates of hell in front of you and open the door to heaven. Enjoy it. Don't be afraid, I'm right here and I know what I'm talking about. You should only feel like this for about another two hours at the most."

"I will close the gates of hell, I will open the gates of heaven," Marie said. "But I know that, even if I can control my fear, you can't control yours. I can see your aura. I can read your thoughts."

"You're right. But then you must also have read that you don't run the least risk of dying from this, unless you decide to climb some building and see if, finally, you're able to fly."

"I understand. Besides, I think it's begun to wear off."

And, knowing she wouldn't die and that the girl at her side would never take her to the top of some building, Marie's speeding heart slowed a bit, and she decided to enjoy the two hours she had left.

All of her senses—touch, sight, hearing smell, taste—became one, as if she were capable of experiencing everything at the same time. The lights outside began to lose their intensity, but even so she could still see the auras of other people. She knew who was suffering, who had found happiness, who would die shortly.

Everything was new. Not only because she was in Istanbul, but because she was in the presence of a Marie she did not know, much more intense and much older than the Marie she had become accustomed to living with for all those years.

The clouds in the sky were growing heavier, warning of a possible storm, and little by little their shapes began to lose the meaning that earlier had been so clear. But she knew that clouds have their own code for speaking with humans, and if she kept an eye on the heavens in the coming days, she would end up learning what they were trying to tell her.

She wondered whether or not to tell her father why she'd chosen to go to Nepal, but it would be silly not to continue on after they'd made it this far. They would discover things that later, with the limitations that came with age, would be more difficult.

How did she know so little about herself? Some unpleasant childhood experiences came back to her, and they now no longer seemed so unpleasant, merely experiences. She had given so much importance to them for so long—why?

But ultimately she didn't need an answer, she could feel these things were resolving themselves. Every now and then, as she looked at what appeared to be spirits circling around her, the gateway to hell passed before her, but she was intent on not opening it.

At that moment, she basked in a world without questions or answers. Without doubts or convictions. She basked in a world that was one with her. She basked in a world without time, where past and future were merely the present, nothing more. At times, her spirit showed itself to be very old; at other times it seemed like a child, making the most of all that was new, looking at her fingers and noticing how they were separate and the way they moved. She watched the girl at her side, happy that she was now much calmer, her light had returned, she really was in love. The question she'd asked earlier made absolutely no sense, we always know when we're in love.

When they came to the door of their hotel, after nearly two hours walking, she knew the Dutch girl had decided they would wander the city so the effects of the drug could pass before they met up with the others. Marie heard the first peal of thunder. She knew that God was talking to her, telling her to come back to the world now, there was much work to be done. She ought to help her father, who dreamed of being a writer but had never committed a single word to paper that wasn't part of a presentation, or a study, or an article.

She needed to help her father as he'd helped her—that was his request. He had many years ahead of him. And one day she would marry, something that had never crossed her mind, and that now she considered the final step in a life without rules or limits.

One day she would marry and her father would need to be content with his own life, doing something he liked to do. She loved her mother very much and didn't blame her for the divorce, but she sincerely wanted her father to find someone with whom to share the steps we all take on this sacred earth.

At that moment, she understood why the drug had been outlawed; the world could only work without it. If it were legal, people would only retreat deeper into themselves, as though they were billions of monks meditating all at the same time in their interior caves, indifferent to the agony and glory of others. Cars would stop working. Planes would never again take off.

There would be no seed or harvest—only awe and ecstasy. In no time, humanity would be swept from the earth by that which in principle could be a purifying breeze but had instead become a gale of collective annihilation.

She was in the world, she belonged to it, and she ought to follow the order God had given her with his thunderous voice—work, help her father, fight against the wrongs she witnessed, engage with others in the daily battles they were fighting.

This was her mission. And she would see it through. She had had her first and last LSD trip, and she was glad it was over.

That night, the same group got together and decided to celebrate their last day in Istanbul at a restaurant that sold alcoholic beverages, where they could eat, get a little drunk together, and share their experiences of the day. Rahul and Michael, the drivers, were invited along. They protested that it was against company protocol, but they soon gave in without much of a fight.

"Don't go asking me to stay another day, I can't do it or I'll lose my job."

The group wasn't asking to stay. There was still much of Turkey ahead of them, especially Anatolia, which everyone said was a marvelous place. The truth was they had begun to miss the constant changes in the landscape.

Paulo had already returned from his mysterious place. He'd gotten dressed for the evening and knew they would be leaving the next day. He begged everyone's forgiveness and explained that he'd like to dine alone with Karla.

Everyone understood and silently rejoiced in that "friendship."

There were two women whose eyes shone bright. Marie and Karla. No one asked why, and neither of them offered any explanations.

How was your day?"

They'd chosen a spot where they could drink, and they'd both already finished their first glass of wine.

Paulo suggested that, before he respond, they order food. Karla agreed. Now that she'd finally become a real woman, capable of loving with all her strength without the aid of some sort of drug, the wine was merely a celebration.

She knew what awaited her. She knew what kind of conversation they would have. She had known ever since they'd made amazing love the night before; at the time, she'd felt like crying, but she accepted her fate as though it were already written. The only thing she'd ever wanted in life was a heart on fire, and the man who'd given her this was at that moment inside her. And that night, when she finally confessed her love, his eyes hadn't lit up as she'd imagined they would.

She wasn't naïve, but she'd always gotten what she wanted in life—she wasn't lost in the desert but running like the waters of the Bosphorus toward a gigantic ocean where all rivers meet, and she would never forget Istanbul, the skinny Brazilian and his conversation, though she couldn't always follow it. He had performed a miracle, but he didn't need to know this—otherwise guilt might change his mind.

They ordered another bottle of wine. It was only then he began to speak.

"The man without a name was at the cultural center when I arrived. I greeted him, but he didn't return my greeting; his eyes were fixed on something, like in a sort of trance. I kneeled on the floor, tried to clear my mind and meditate, to reach out to the souls there who danced about, singing and celebrating life. I knew that at some point he would leave his state, and I waited—actually, I didn't 'wait' in the literal sense of the term, I delivered myself to the present moment, without waiting for absolutely anything.

"The loudspeakers called the city to prayer, the man returned from his trance state and performed one of that day's five rituals. It was only then he noticed I was there. He asked why I'd returned.

"I explained that I'd spent the night thinking about our previous encounter and that I'd like to deliver myself, body and soul, to Sufism. I was dying to tell him how, for the first time in my life, I'd made love—because when we were in bed, and I was inside you, it was as though I really was leaving my own body. I'd never experienced that before. But I deemed the subject inappropriate and said nothing.

" 'Read the poets,' came the response from the man without a name. 'That's all you'll ever need.'

"That wasn't all I needed. I needed discipline, rigor, a place to serve God so that I could be closer to the rest of the world.

Before going there for the first time, I had been fascinated by the dervishes who danced and entered into a sort of trance. Now I needed my soul to dance with me.

"I ought to wait a thousand and one days so this could happen? Perfect, I'd wait. By that time, I'd done plenty of living—perhaps twice as much as my high school classmates. I could dedicate the next three years of my life and, eventually, try to enter into that perfect trance of the dancing dervishes.

"'My friend, a Sufi is a person who lives in the present moment. *Tomorrow* isn't a part of our vocabulary.'

"Yes, that I knew. My real question was whether I needed to convert to Islam to continue my learning.

"'No. You need make only one promise: deliver yourself to the path of God. See His face each time you drink a cup of water. Listen to His voice each time you pass a beggar on the street. That's what every religion teaches and it's the only promise we ought to make—the only one.'

"'I still lack the discipline for that, but with your help I'll arrive at the place where heaven meets earth—in man's heart.'

"The man without a name said that he could help me if I left my entire life behind and did everything he told me. Learn to beg when I had no money, to fast when the moment arrived, to serve lepers, to wash the wounds of the sick. To spend my days doing absolutely nothing, merely staring at a fixed point and repeating the same mantra, the same phrase, the same word.

"'Sell your wisdom and buy space in your soul to be filled with the Absolute. Because the wisdom of men and women is madness before God.'

"At that moment, I began to doubt I was capable of this—

275

perhaps he was testing me with this demand for absolute obedience. But I detected no hesitation in his voice, I knew he was serious. I also knew that my body had entered that green room that was falling apart, with its broken stained glass and on that day particularly free of filtering light, as a storm was approaching.

"I knew that my body had entered that place, but my soul had remained outside, waiting to see what would come of it all. Waiting for the day when, by a simple coincidence, I would walk in there and see others spinning around one another. Everything would be a well-orchestrated ballet and nothing else. But that wasn't what I was looking for.

"I knew that if I didn't accept the conditions he was imposing at that moment, the next time I'd find the door closed to me—even if I could come and go as I pleased, as I'd done the first time.

"The man was reading my soul, observing my contradictions and doubts, and at no moment did he show any flexibility—it was all or nothing. He said he needed to return to his special meditation, and I asked him to answer at least three more questions.

" 'Do you accept me as your disciple?'

" 'I accept your heart as a disciple, because I cannot refuse—otherwise, my life would have no use. I have two ways of showing my love of God: the first is to praise Him day and night, in the solitude of this room, but that wouldn't be the least use to me or Him. The second is to sing, dance, and show His face to all through my joy.'

" 'Do you accept me as your disciple?' I asked a second time.

" 'A bird cannot fly with a single wing. A Sufi teacher is nothing if he cannot share his experience with someone else.'

" 'Do you accept me as your disciple?' I asked for the third and final time.

" 'If tomorrow you come in through that door as you've done the last two days, I accept you as my disciple. But I'm almost certain you'll regret it.' "

Karla filled up their glasses again and toasted with Paulo.

"My journey ended here," he repeated, perhaps thinking she hadn't understood what he'd just told her. "I don't have anything to do in Nepal."

He steadied himself for the tears, the fury, the despair, the emotional manipulation, everything to be said by the woman who had told him "I love you" the night before.

But she just smiled.

"I never thought I'd be capable of loving someone the way I love you," Karla responded after they'd emptied their glasses and she'd filled them one more time. "My heart was locked up, and it had nothing to do with psychologists, a lack of chemical substances, that sort of thing. It's something I'll never be able to explain, but suddenly, I don't know exactly the moment, my heart opened. And I'm going to love you for the rest of my life. When I'm in Nepal, I'll be loving you. When I return to Amsterdam, I'll be loving you. When I finally fall for someone else, I'll continue loving you, even if in a different way from today.

"God—I don't know if He exists but I know I hope He's here with us now, listening to my words—I ask to never again allow me to be satisfied with only my own company. That I never feel afraid of needing someone or of suffering, because there is no suffering worse than the dark, gray room where pain cannot reach.

"And that this love so many people speak of, so many share, so many suffer on account of, that this love lead me to that which was unknown and is now becoming clearer. That, as a poet once said, He takes me to a world where there exists no sun, no moon, no stars, no earth, not even the taste of wine in my mouth, merely the Other, he whom I will find because you opened the way.

"That I might walk without need of my feet, see without needing to look, fly without asking for wings."

Paulo was surprised and content at the same time. Both of them were coming to an unknown place, with its terrors and its wonders. There, in Istanbul—a place where they might have visited the many attractions that had been suggested to them—they'd chosen to journey into their own souls and there was nothing better or more comforting than this.

He got up, walked around the table, and kissed her, knowing it was against the local custom, that the owners might be offended—despite this, he kissed her with love and not lust, with pleasure and not guilt, because he knew that it would be their last kiss.

He didn't want to ruin the magic of the moment, but he needed to ask all the same.

"Were you expecting that? Were you prepared for that?"

Karla didn't respond, merely smiled, and he would never know her response—and that was true love, a question for which there is no answer.

He made a point of walking her to the bus. He'd already advised the driver that he was staying behind, to learn what he needed to learn. For a brief moment, he thought to repeat the famous line from *Casablanca,* "We'll always have Paris." But he knew it was a silly idea, and he needed to hurry back to the green room and the teacher without a name.

The people on the bus pretended not to see anything. No one said goodbye to him because no one—besides the driver—knew this was the last stop on his journey.

Karla hugged him without a word but could feel his love as though it were something physical, a light growing more intense, as though the morning sun were rising and shining first across the mountains, then the cities, then the plains, then the sea.

The door closed and the bus took off. More than one person could be heard exclaiming, "Hey, you left the Brazilian guy behind!" But the bus had already pulled away.

One day he would meet Karla again and ask about the rest of her journey.

Epilogue

In February 2005, when he was already a world-famous writer, Paulo went to Amsterdam to give an important talk. On the morning of the talk, he was interviewed on one of Holland's principal TV shows at his old hostel—since converted into a hotel for nonsmokers, expensive and with a small but well-regarded high-end restaurant.

He never again heard from Karla. The guide *Europe on 5 Dollars a Day* had become *Europe on 30 Dollars a Day*. Paradiso had closed (it would reopen a few years later, retaining its identity as a concert venue); Dam Square was deserted, it was merely a square with that mysterious obelisk in the middle, whose purpose he'd never known—and which he would prefer never to know.

He felt the temptation to walk through the streets where they'd walked to reach the restaurant where they'd eaten for free, but there was always someone with him—the person who had organized the talk. He thought it better to return to his hotel and prepare what he was to say that evening.

He had a vague hope that Karla, knowing he was in the city,

would show up to meet him. He imagined she hadn't spent much time in Nepal, just as he'd abandoned the idea of becoming a Sufi, though he'd lasted nearly a year and learned things he would carry with him for the rest of his life.

During the conference, he told part of the story found in this book. At a certain point, he couldn't help it and asked:

"Karla, are you here?"

No one raised a hand. Perhaps she had been there, perhaps she hadn't even heard that he would be visiting the city, or perhaps she was there but preferred not to relive the past.

Better that way.

Geneva, February 3, 2018

Author's Note and Acknowledgments

All of the characters in this book are real but—with the exception of two—had their names changed due to the complete impossibility of finding them (I knew them only by their first names).

I took the episode from the prison at Ponta Grossa (in 1968) and added details from two others to which I was subjected during the military dictatorship (in May 1974, when I was working as a songwriter).

I would like to thank my editor, Matinas Suzuki, Jr.; my agent and friend, Monica Antunes; and my wife, the visual artist Christina Oiticica (who drew the map of the complete Magic Bus route). When I write a book, I lock myself in and practically speak to no one, and I don't like to talk about what I'm writing. Christina pretends not to know, and I pretend to believe that she doesn't know.

**Sometimes you have to lose yourself to discover
who you really are.**

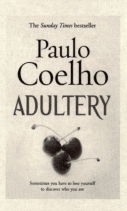

Linda knows she's lucky. Yet every morning when she opens her
eyes to a so-called new day, she feels like closing them again.

Her friends recommend medication but Linda wants to feel more,
not less.

And so she embarks on an adventure as unexpected as it is
daring, which reawakens a side of her that she – respectable wife,
loving mother, ambitious journalist – thought had disappeared.

'*Adultery* perfectly illustrates the faint line between madness and
insanity, happiness and unhappiness.'
Daily Express

arrow books

The unforgettable story of a woman who dared to break the conventions of her time – and paid the price.

When Mata Hari arrived in Paris, she had nothing yet she soon became known as the most elegant woman in the city.

Dancer, courtesan and confidante, she delighted her audiences and bewitched the era's most powerful men. But as paranoia consumed a country at war, Mata Hari's lifestyle brought her under suspicion and in 1917, she was arrested, accused of espionage.

Told in Mata Hari's voice, *The Spy* is an unforgettable story of a woman whose only crime was her defiant independence.

'Beautifully written and gripping.'
Sunday Mirror

arrow books